Ceiling Stars

Ceiling Stars

Sandra Diersch

James Lorimer & Company Ltd., Publishers
Toronto

First publication in the United States, 2004

James Lorimer & Company Ltd. acknowledges the support of the Ontario Arts Council. We acknowledge the support of the Government of Canada through the Book Publishing Industry Development Program (BPIDP) for our publishing activities. We acknowledge the support of the Canada Council for the Arts for our publishing program. We acknowledge the support of the Government of Ontario through the Ontario Media Development Corporation's Ontario Book Initiative.

Cover design: Clarke MacDonald

Canada Cataloguing in Publication Data

Diersch, Sandra
    Ceiling stars / written by Sandra Diersch.

(SideStreets)
ISBN 1-55028-835-0 (bound).—ISBN 1-55028-834-2 (pbk.)

I. Title. II. Series.

PS8557.I385C43 2004   jC813'.54   C2004-900479-4

James Lorimer & Company Ltd., Publishers 35 Britain Street Toronto, Ontario M5A 1R7 www.lorimer.ca	Distributed in the United States by: Orca Book Publishers, P.O. Box 468 Custer, WA USA 98240-0468 Printed and bound in Canada

For my mother, who was there and knows.
And for Chris and my beautiful Jenna
with so much love.

Special thanks to Ellen, Joan, Nan
and Shelley for reading the manuscript and
offering their suggestions and professional
support. To my editor Hadley and her staff
for helping me shape and polish this book
into the story I wanted to tell.

Chapter 1

"Did you see this, Chris? This is so wondrous! Did you see it?" my best friend, Danelle Mueller cries, descending on me in the hot, over-crowded cafeteria. A piece of coloured paper flutters in her hand. Some kids at the next table look up from their plates of fries and gravy to stare at Danelle, but she is oblivious.

"How can I see it when you're waving it in my face?" I ask.

"Burnt Toast is going to be downtown next Thursday signing autographs! Isn't that chimerical? Of course, we have to go."

Chimerical? What the hell does that mean? Danelle has obviously been reading the thesaurus, a habit of hers.

"We have school," I remind her, thinking of January exams in two weeks, and graduation looming on the horizon.

"This is Burnt Toast, *Burnt Toast*. We have all

their CDs. We have to go," Danelle tells me, still shaking the poster in my face.

Her long dark hair has come loose from its knot and strands stick in her mouth as she talks. She pulls them away impatiently, and then stops fluttering the paper to show it to me. Her eyes are very green and very bright, and she dances a little two-step.

I am not good at breaking the rules. Danelle has known this since that October day in grade seven when we first met. She tried to convince me to go to the corner store at lunch and I stood arguing with her about it for so long a supervisor noticed. Danelle would have been suspended for breaking school rules for the third time (she'd already left the grounds once that fall, and she climbed the roof of the school to retrieve a ball) if I hadn't made up a story about an injured stray dog we were trying to capture. That was the beginning of my career in fiction and my friendship with Danelle.

However, I remind myself, snapping back to the present, she has a point. I have memorized nearly every one of Burnt Toast's songs. Getting an autograph would be so totally cool.

"Why don't you take my copy and get it signed for me?"

"No way. You have to go with me. Come on!" she pleads, flopping onto the chair beside me.

She grabs my hands, holding them tightly in her own, and leans in close enough that I can smell the stale cigarette smoke trapped in the fabric of her clothes and hanging from every word she speaks. I wrinkle my nose.

"The truant officers aren't going to come looking for you," she tells me. "You could use a day off from your pedestrian existence. It'll be fun. There'll be multitudes of people there who should be in school."

My head is spinning. It's so much easier to go along with the rules, to conform. I don't know where this attitude of mine came from, my sister certainly doesn't have it, and it's not like my parents are super strict or anything. It's just boring old Christine Dawson and her uptight little personality, I guess.

"I have assignments and stuff."

"Hand them in after lunch — it's not like we'll be gone all day. Relax, Chris! It's not the end of the world. And this is Burnt Toast!"

I look up at Danelle and suddenly I hear myself caving in. Danelle whoops loudly, hugs me, then takes up her dancing again, singing snatches of songs from the latest Burnt Toast CD, filling in with humming when she doesn't know the words. "This is going to be so cool! I'm so glad you decided to come with me!"

"Can I finish my lunch now?" I ask, but I'm not hungry anymore. I am already imagining the hell there will be to pay when someone finds out.

* * *

Danelle talks about our little "adventure" all the way home, but I hardly hear her as we pick our way over partially frozen puddles and the remains of snow. January is not a pretty month in Richmond. To get to my house we have to pass through a rundown section of town that looks awful all the time, but even fancy landscaping and stamped concrete driveways would look horrible under melting snow.

When we get to the house Danelle flops onto my bed and closes her eyes.

"I'm really glad you agreed to go with me, Chris," she says. "I know we'll have a riotous time. Especially if you stop worrying about it." She opens one eye and smiles at me.

"I'll try. Do you remember that guy, Brad, from French?" I ask.

"The one who's been eyeballing you since November? Did he finally ask you out?" She sits up, crosses her legs, and looks expectantly at me.

"Right. Like that's ever going to happen."

"What happened? He was certainly giving all the signals."

"You won't believe this, but he already has a girlfriend. She lives in Vancouver."

"What a bastard! He was flirting with you for weeks! I'll start a smear campaign first thing tomorrow," my best friend promises, and I feel myself grinning. "Should we start saying he's got some STD? What would be a good one?"

I am laughing now, although not all the sting of

my disappointment has gone. "I think he should have herpes and gonorrhea, and B.O. The whole works."

"I'm sorry, Chris," she tells me with a small smile. "But I have something that might make you feel better."

Danelle digs into the pocket of her jean jacket and pulls out a thin package. She flashes it at me as she rips it open. A sheet of stickers falls on the bed. They're fluorescent yellow stars.

"I painted the walls of my room this intense shade of blue last night and put the stars on the ceiling. It is just so fierce. I love it. My father kind of freaked, but what could he do when I'd already painted?"

"You want to put yellow stickers on my ceiling?"

"Yeah! Then at night, when they're glowing, you can think of me in my room and it'll be like we're closer. It would be a cementing of our friendship. Like those friendship bracelets we made at camp when we were thirteen. You know the ones with the beads and our names spelled out?"

"I remember."

"It could be great. And if you really don't like it, you could take them off, right? It isn't as though they're permanent."

She seems completely oblivious to the fact that the very thing that is supposed to cement our friendship isn't permanent. But I don't bother to point it out to her.

"Pretend you're a Bohemian living in a loft in

Soho trying to be true to your art," Danelle tells me, taking my hand. She moves me around the room as she talks, painting pictures with her words. In a few seconds my ordinary suburban bedroom, with the gingham curtains and Irish chain quilt, has been transformed into a writer's loft.

"There are no walls in this loft, only space and light and texture," Danelle says softly. "Great, soft, brightly coloured pillows on the floor, candles and flowers in bowls, and obscure prints on the walls. And a galaxy of stars to remind you of the infinite power of the universe."

I pull away from her, laughing so hard my sides hurt. I can't even stop when I look up and see the hurt expression on her face. "I'm sorry! I am. It's just … ooh, I hurt," I say, doubling over. "It's just too much. Fine, we'll put the stars on the ceiling. But please, no more lofts in Soho. I couldn't live like that."

In a flash Danelle has her shoes off and is standing on my bed, critically analyzing my ceiling.

When she's done we lie side by side on my bed, staring up at the results of her labour. Danelle has made the room as dark as she can and the stars actually glow — kind of weakly, but they do glow.

"It looks good," I tell her, surprised at how much I like it.

"See? Didn't I tell you? I love mine. And now when we go to bed, we can think of each other lying under the same big sky. Isn't there some kind of song about that? From some Disney movie

I think. Anyway, they look good."

I glance sideways at her; she takes my hand and squeezes it. We lie there together, staring at my ceiling. Everyone should have a friend like Danelle, I think: someone who pushes you out of your comfort zone. I don't always feel this way — in fact, usually it's the exact opposite — but right now, staring at my "galaxy," I squeeze her hand back.

Chapter 2

"Burnt Toast is going to be downtown signing autographs next week," I say to my friend Jack as he
and I leave school together the next day. "Danelle's
talked me into going with her."

I am curious how he'll react to this news. Jack
is pretty much the opposite of Danelle. My friendship with Jack is much calmer than when Danelle
and I are together, which is definitely a nice
change sometimes.

"Really? You, skipping school?"

He pushes his blonde hair out of his eyes, only
to have it fall back, like a curtain shielding his
eyes from me. In the four years I've known him,
he's shot up in height and put on no weight. He's
skinny and he slouches when he walks, like a car-
toon character of a teenaged boy, but he has the
most amazing brown eyes and a killer smile. Plus,
even though he's an artist, he is so completely not
"arty." His favourite clothes are an old pair of

faded jeans, his brown leather boots, and shirts with button-down collars. I bought him a beret once as a joke, but he refuses to wear it.

"I know, bizarre, eh?" I shrug. "The things a girl will do for a brush with celebrity."

We wait at the corner for the light to change before crossing. Even then, as Jack steps off the curb he's nearly taken out by some jerk running the light. He gives the driver the finger, then turns to grin at me.

"So, if I give you a copy of my CD, would you get it signed for me?"

"You could come along. I think it is only one per customer or something."

"Figures they'd do it on a school day, hey? Naw, I can't go. I have a huge project due that morning in art class. You go be a rebel," he says. "I'll be the good boy."

"Yeah, right. Jack Bellows, Boy Scout," I say, scuffing my sneaker on the sidewalk. I can just hear my mother's voice telling me to pick up my feet. "Did I tell you I got those poems back from Ms. Armstrong today?"

"And?"

"I'm sticking to fiction. She didn't come right out and say it, but she pretty much hinted that they stunk."

"You should have let me read them before you handed them in. I might have been able to help."

I don't answer him. I have never shown anyone my writing. Ever. Except for assignments for creative writing class, I'm the only one who sees my work. It's better that way. If it stinks, no one has to know but me. I love my teacher, but her habit of making us try new things drives me crazy. She's always getting us to "push the envelope" and "flex our creative muscles," which for me has resulted in some pretty amazing garbage.

We reach my house and I start digging around in my backpack for my keys. "Why is it that you and Danelle always end up here?" I mutter. "Is there something wrong with your houses?"

"Your house is clean."

This is definitely true. Although, to be fair, Jack's mother works full time and has two teenaged sons and a daughter living with her. How clean could their house be?

We head straight for the kitchen. I pick up the note from the table and read it as I shrug out of my coat.

"Mom took Katie to the orthodontist. I'm supposed to order pizza later. Wanna stay?" I ask Jack as we scrounge around for something to eat. I throw him an apple from the bowl on the counter and grab a bag of sour-cream-and-onion chips from the pantry. Armed with snacks, we go down to the rec room and turn on the television.

"I think Dad is taking me, Mark, and Carina out for dinner tonight," he says, swallowing half the apple in one bite. Jack and his brother and sister spend alternate weekends with their dad and his wife, Jessica.

"Is it his weekend to have you? How can we go out tomorrow if you're going to be in Cloverdale?"

We get settled on the couch and I put the bag of potato chips between us.

"He's taking Carina and Mark back with him, but I'm not going."

"Oh, yeah?" I ask, casually. The divorce wasn't a nice one when it happened just after I met Jack, and ever since he hasn't been thrilled about his dad.

"He's a little dictator about it all, you know?" he says, crunching loudly. "Everything planned to the last second. I'm too old for that crap.

"Last time we were out there, before Christmas, Jessica blew up because I refused to go do whatever lame-ass activity Dad planned. She was even wagging her finger in my face like I was ten or something."

He gets up to pace around the room. I turn off the TV and wait for him to continue.

"So I told her I had three assignments the next week and couldn't afford to spend the day doing whatever Dad had planned. The rest of them could go without me. I even offered to cook dinner. No deal. She said I was ungrateful and didn't give a damn about anyone's feelings but my own. So I told her where to go. Then Dad had an absolute freak and told me to pack my bag and go home, and then Carina started crying. It stank."

Jack is over in the corner by the easy chair. He runs his hand through his hair three times quickly.

The third time he leaves it there, pulling his bangs back from his eyes. He looks at me, but I'm not sure he sees me. The furnace clicks on and our neighbour's dog barks.

"Did you leave?"

Jack is startled. He had forgotten I was there, I think. He shakes his head slowly. "Naw. We all calmed down and Dad and I had a talk. We worked it out, or partially anyway. He's not thrilled that I won't come on his weekends, but I guess he figures he doesn't have a choice anymore. I'll come when my schedule lets me, which means when I feel like it. And he says he'll make more of an effort to get in touch during the week. Maybe get tickets to a Canucks game." Jack shrugs and makes his way back over to the couch. He falls into the cushions and puts an arm over his eyes.

"The truth is," he says a second later, moving his arm to look at me. "I'd rather spend the time with Mom's boyfriend, Nick. My dad is too caught up in parenting. He figures he's gotta cram all his 'father' stuff into weekends and he never just lets himself have fun with us."

"Did you tell him that? To cool out?"

"Naw, why bother?"

He reaches his hand into the chip bag and then just stares at the food lying on his hand, as if he is unsure what to do with it. "What kind of crap is there to watch on this thing?" he asks, grabbing the remote from the couch and clicking on the TV.

"I had a big fight with my mom last week, actually, about kind of the same thing," I say a little later, wanting to even things out a bit. "My grandparents had this big thing at their curling club and families were invited. It was last weekend and I was swamped with school stuff, so I said I couldn't go. Mom had a freak. Lots of talk about disappointing people and budgeting my time better. Blah, blah."

"Did you go?"

"No. But I called my grandmother and told her why I wasn't coming. Of course she understood. She even said Mom didn't need to get so upset."

"Parents get so intense about the stupidest things."

"Tell me about it."

Jack leaves when I get up to call for the pizza. "So, I guess I'll see you tomorrow night, then?"

"Yeah. Good luck with dinner tonight."

"Hey," he says, moving away from the door to face me. I look up at him, waiting. "About all this — everything is fine. You know that, right? I mean, we'll work it out, me and my dad."

"Yeah, I know."

"Anyway. Thanks. I'll see ya 'round." He reaches for the door, then suddenly turns and grabs me, pulling me into a tight hug. My arms go around him automatically and we stand there for a second. I can feel our hearts pounding against each other's chest. He pulls away first and is out the door before I can react. I close the door behind him and slump against it.

Chapter 3

Danelle and I catch the bus Thursday morning to go downtown. All the arranging and planning and secret phone calls have left me a nervous wreck. By the time we are on the bus, I am close to throwing up.

"This is just so completely awesome!" she keeps mumbling, nudging me with her shoulder or elbow.

I look out the window, pretending to myself that I am actually on my way to school. My insides are mush. I couldn't eat breakfast — I couldn't even say good-bye to my mother. No one needs to tell me that I'm pathetic.

"Did you bring your CD? You remembered it, didn't you?" Danelle asks, leaning over me to pull open my backpack.

"Get out of there!" I snap, grabbing it away from her. "God, would you calm down?" Her hyperactivity is not helping my nerves. "Yeah, I brought it."

"This is so great! We'll probably have to wait a bit for the store to open but we should have a good place in line. And then we can go back to school so you don't have a major heart attack or something," she says, making a face at me.

"Just for kicks, sometime you should come to school with me, attend some classes, live on the edge a bit," I say, but Danelle has recognized someone she knows and is halfway down the bus aisle, calling to them. It is going to be a long morning.

We finally get off the bus and then have to walk a few blocks, surrounded by the throngs of people heading for their offices.

"Can you imagine spending nine hours of your day, five days a week behind one of those windows?" I ask, pointing up to one of the office towers.

Danelle makes a face. "I can hardly manage six hours of school a day. Thank God I'm going on the stage. No offices for me, just walking the boards."

"Spare change?" a voice asks.

We are stopped at a corner, waiting for the light to change. I look into the eyes of a girl who is about the same age as my sister. Her hair, partially hidden beneath a colourful but very dirty hat, is lank, her face is dirty, and she smells of unwashed flesh. I shake my head and look away.

Danelle has her bag open and is rummaging in it for coins. The light changes and all around us people move off the sidewalk. Danelle finds her wallet and opens it. The girl holds out her hand, wrapped in a glove with the fingers cut away. Danelle pulls out a ten-dollar bill.

"Stock up, okay?" she says, touching the girl's shoulder. The girl pulls back as though she's been slapped, then shoves the money in her pocket and turns away. She goes about two steps, then turns back.

"Thanks," she says, and is gone.

"That was really generous," I tell her. "I always get so embarrassed by street people."

"Could be you or me just as easily."

"I know. But still. You could have given her a dollar. Ten bucks is a lot."

I get no answer and turn to look at her. She's blushing. "What?"

"Can you lend me money for the bus home?" she asks. I nearly trip over a curb laughing.

* * *

When I come home that afternoon, my sister is sitting at the kitchen table, eating a bowl of cereal and reading a book. I am still feeling flushed with my little act of rebellion. My signed CD is tucked safely in my backpack. One of the band members even shook my hand. I grunt a hello at Katie as I kick off my shoes and hang up my coat, then I head up to my room.

Katie used to be this neat little kid, kind of funny

looking but interesting to talk to and really bright. When she turned thirteen, however, some kind of hormonal imbalance took place and overnight she turned into this freaky twit. Her blonde hair has been cut almost completely off and what is left is jet black and clipped all over with little metallic clips. Her clothing consists of concert T-shirts, grungy jeans, and an old pair of high tops.

She follows me upstairs and leans against the door jam, her arms folded across her chest. She's wearing my Burnt Toast T-shirt. I am immediately suspicious.

"Take off my clothes, you little brat, and stop stealing things out of my closet."

"You can have your shirt," she tells me with a smirk. "What I want to know is who convinced you to skip today and go downtown? I bet it was Danelle. She'd be about the only one who could convince Prissy Chrissy to skip school. So where is it?" She takes a step forward.

"Come on, show me the CD. You got it signed, didn't you?"

I have an incredible urge to smack her. How the hell did she find out? "I'm not showing you anything. Get out."

"Melissa saw you at the record store this morning," Katie tells me, perching on my bed. "So what I want to know is, how much is it worth to you for me to keep my mouth shut?"

"Give me my shirt and get the hell out of my room."

"Here's your bloody shirt," she says, standing up to peel the T-shirt over her head. She stands in the middle of my room in her bra and jeans, and grins at me again.

"You know, it's pretty funny, actually," she says. "I told Melissa she must have been mistaken because my big sister is so anal about being good and doing what she's told, she would never skip. But Melissa said she was absolutely sure it was you, and you were with a dark-haired girl who never stopped talking. Who else could it be but you and that twit Danelle?"

"GET OUT NOW!" I scream at her, grabbing at her scrawny arm to haul her to the door. She wrenches free of my hand and shoves at me.

"I'm going! But think about what I know, sister."

I slam the door behind her and lean against it, trying to think. She'll tell — I have no doubt about that. We take turns snitching on each other, and it's her turn since I nailed her over Christmas break when she was out way past her curfew.

The phone rings. It's Jack. "So, how was it?" he asks.

"No 'hello, how are you?'"

"No. How was it? You get it signed? Did you nearly go into cardiac arrest from skipping?"

"Ha ha. As a matter of fact, I had a great time and got all four guys to sign it. One of them even kissed me!"

"You're a liar," he tells me good-naturedly. "Well, now that your quota for rebellious acts has been reached for the year, what now?"

"You're not funny, and if I didn't need your advice really badly right now, I'd hang up." I fill him in on Katie's little extortion scheme. Jack howls on the other end of the phone.

"That little cow," he says when he can breathe again. "What are you going to do?"

"What can I do? I could tell my parents first, take away her joy in snitching."

"Or," Jack says slowly, "you could blackmail her into keeping quiet. I happen to know that yesterday it was your sister who was not where she was supposed to be."

Jack gives me the details and I go in hunt of my precious sister. I find her curled up on the sofa in front of the TV. She grins at me as I come down the stairs.

"Ready to deal?" she asks.

"Sure," I tell her, getting comfy in the recliner. "How about I'll show you my signed CD, and you show me your tattoo."

Katie's black-rimmed eyes widen in disbelief and her already pale skin becomes whiter. Her mouth opens and closes again. She looks like a guppy.

"Come on, let me see it! It's on your back, isn't it? Is it a little dragon to go with your collection? I hope you went some place that was clean, at least."

Chapter 4

"I am going up on the roof," Danelle informs me.

We have been sitting at the computer in Danelle's bedroom, looking at websites on astronomy. Images of the Milky Way are floating on the screen.

"The roof? Seriously?"

Danelle's house is quite high and there are lots of gables and peaks on the roof. It is not a place I'd want to be climbing on a dark, frosty night.

"Why not? I'll be able to see the stars much better from up there. I might even be able to see this," she says, pointing to the computer. "Come with me."

She has shut down the computer and is already halfway out the door. I follow, intrigued as usual by my friend's ideas and her immediate ability to turn words into actions. But there's no way I am following her up to the roof.

She finds a ladder in the garage and carries it

out to the backyard. The January night is deeply, coldly dark, and I wrap my arms around myself for warmth.

"You hold the ladder for me, okay?" Danelle says, testing the balance before starting her climb. My heart is beating quickly as I watch her rear end disappear above me. At the top, she carefully pulls herself over the eave then sits for a second, looking down. She grins at me and waves. I wave back.

"Will you come up?"

"Not a chance," I say, squinting to see her in the dim light from the porch.

"I want to see everything. I'm going a little higher."

My hands have grown icy holding the metal edges of the ladder, so I let go and stick them in my pockets. I know Danelle shouldn't be up there, but as long as she stays where she can hold on she should be okay. I take a few steps backward to look up, and finally find her. She's sitting on one side of the gables.

"Come on, join me! It is so prodigious up here!" she cries out of the darkness.

Prodigious: one of her favourite words. She thinks the word "interesting" is far too "pedestrian" and refuses to use it. But just now I don't care how prodigious or interesting or whatever it is up there, I'm starting to get scared. I notice the frost on the grass — if there's frost down here, there's definitely frost up there.

"Danelle, maybe you should come down now," I call. "It's starting to freeze. You could slip."

She waves at me, then spreads her arms wide and throws her head back. "I could see forever up here if it was still light out. Over there is the school, and Monty's store. It feels like it might snow — that'd be cool, eh? It's almost February and we still haven't had much."

She climbs up even higher and starts walking along the highest edge, arms stretched out for balance. My fear is growing and I feel like I might cry. Some of the stunts she has been pulling lately have been pretty weird, but this is just dangerous.

"Please come down, Danelle," I call out.

"COOL!" she cries, reaching the chimney and grabbing on. "Did you see that?" she calls down to me. "There was a shooting star! I wish the power would go out — then we'd really see the stars.

"I'm going to find a galaxy of my own, name it, and register it. And maybe one day I'll get to space and actually see it up close and everything. Wouldn't it be cool to be an astronaut? Even an astronomer. I'm a Pisces, which is a water sign, but I think I should have been born under a different sign. I don't think I was born right. I should have been an Aries or something."

"Do you want to be an astronomer or an astrologer?" I ask, not that I care. I just want to keep contact — and to get her down from there.

"I'm getting cold, Danelle," I call up to her. "Will you come down now so we can go in?"

"Hey, I think I just saw Billy Anderson and Parma Grewal making out! Isn't she dating some guy from Vancouver? A football player or something…"

"Danelle, how about we go in and make some popcorn and watch the movie? It's really cold out here," I try again but she ignores me. "If you don't come down now, Danelle, I'm calling the fire department."

"Don't you dare! Christine Dawson, if you do, I'll never speak to you again as long as I live!" she screams at me, still gripping the chimney.

I look up at her, my heart pounding in my ears. "I don't care, Danelle. I'd rather have you alive and not talking to me than dead and not talking to me."

A bat or an owl flies past. Danelle is startled by the *whoosh* so close to her head and she jumps. I scream as she slides down the far side of the roof, disappearing from my sight. Frantically I run around the house, struggling with the gate.

By the time I make it to the front of the house she has steadied herself and is sitting on the edge of the roof, her feet dangling from the eaves.

"See, all in one piece," she says, her breath hard and fast. Her hair is wild around her head. In the dim glow from the street lamp her face is pale. She was scared, I realize. Finally, finally she was scared. "No need for a fire department rescue. Although being carried down a ladder by a hunky firefighter would not be a bad thing at all."

She waits while I bring the ladder around, then

she turns carefully and finds the rungs with her feet. Once she is safely on the ground again, I start my lecture.

"You could have fallen! You could have broken your neck and your back, every bone in your body! You could have killed yourself!"

Danelle laughs at me and shakes her head. "I didn't fall. It was great! I wonder if I was a bird in a past life or something. I just love to not feel encumbered by anything, you know?" She asks me the question, but isn't really interested in my answer. By the time we head inside and up to her room, I've calmed down a bit.

"I have to tell you what happened after we went downtown last week," I say when we get to her room. "Katie found out somehow—"

Danelle cuts in as if she doesn't hear me, "The other night I had a dream that I was flying. Actually I wasn't really flying, it was more like floating. I was just suspended in space and I would just think about moving and I would. I'm almost sure it was an out-of-body experience. The stars seemed close enough to touch, and there were so many of them! I wish you could have been with me." She goes to the stereo.

"Danelle, I was trying to tell you something," I say, but I am distracted by the pulsing sounds coming from the speakers. "What is with this music?"

She is lighting dozens of candles and a couple of incense sticks. With her dark walls, the stars shimmering overhead, and the smell of incense floating around us, the whole evening has taken on a slightly surreal tone.

"Isn't it so completely cool?" she asks jumping onto her bed and crossing her legs. She closes her eyes and sways slightly to the strange sounds. "It is African tribal music, or something like that. I got it the other day when I was at the mall. I love it."

I don't like it. It bangs around in my head, thumping and thudding like someone hitting me with a hammer. It makes me feel jumpy and uneasy.

"As I was saying, Katie found out we skipped and she tried to blackmail me but Jack found out…"

"I know I put it under here. I remember doing it. Where the hell is it?" Danelle mutters, screwing up her face as her arm slides from side to side under the pillow. "If my mother was in here, going through my things, I'll kill her," she goes on, scowling. "Stupid woman is always prowling around where she isn't supposed to."

"Danelle, I am trying to tell you something. Will you stop interrupting me, please?" I say, but she is intent on what she's doing.

"I've been waiting all day for this," she says, pulling a joint out from under her pillow. She lights the end and takes a deep drag. She closes her eyes and the smoke slowly leaks from the corner of her mouth, joining the smoke from the candles and incense. The smoke moves in my direction and I get a whiff of the slightly sweet scent.

"Would you like to try?" she offers, holding it out to me.

"No, thanks."

"Prisssy Chrissssy." Danelle takes another drag before putting it out. She closes her eyes and lets the smoke slowly escape from her mouth, as if she has done this thousands of times. For all I know, she has.

She slides off the bed and crawls across the floor to my cushion. She kneels in front of me, her brown eyes narrow slits. "Are you sure you wouldn't like to try? Just one drag? Live a little," she whispers. "It won't hurt you. It will…free you."

She is smiling at me, her eyes shining brightly. Her breath is warm in my face. "It won't hurt you, I promise," she says, her voice still soft. She moves closer to me and holds the lighter out, the little flame dancing between us. Her eyes hold mine for a long, long second as she lights the joint again.

Chapter 5

Danelle is not at our usual meeting spot Monday morning, but I find her at our lockers when I get to school. She is wearing some incredibly bizarre outfit I'm sure she found at a rummage sale — long flowered skirt, over-sized man's shirt, and big black boots — and she has her hair piled high on her head. She throws her arms around me and hugs me hard.

"Wasn't Saturday night fun? We have to do that again," she begins. She is so in my face, I take several steps away from her.

We will definitely not be doing that again soon. Danelle spent the rest of the night hearing her mother coming up the stairs, her father at the window. Twice she made me go outside and check for footprints in the garden. Her paranoia drove me nuts. She was acting strange before she smoked the pot, and she definitely got worse after. I'm beginning to wonder if she's doing more than just dope, but I'm so amazingly ignorant about drugs that I wouldn't know what or how or anything.

"I did absolutely nothing yesterday. I didn't even get dressed! I watched the movie again, wasn't it good? So much was going on I couldn't take it all in the first time."

"It was a good movie, if you had shut up and let me watch it—"

"I thought I might go for a bike ride, but then it started raining and I decided I'd just get wet so I stayed in. And it was a good thing I did, because you'll never guess who called!"

Of course I know who called: Brian Foster, God's gift to humanity and Danelle's on-again, off-again boyfriend for the last year and a half. He's a complete zero. He graduated from high school two years ago, and has a job and his own place, but he treats Danelle like shit.

"I can't believe it, really, but he did and we're going out this weekend. You know, it's funny because I don't miss him until he calls and then he calls and I realize, 'Hey, I miss you! Let's get together!'"

"Do you think that's such a good idea?" I ask. "I mean, last time he cheated on you, Danelle, remember? And I think he's using crack or something…"

"We'll see how it goes. But I think maybe this time it will be better. I mean, he must really care about me, right? Because he's so persistent. And he really isn't as bad as he comes across. If you got to know him a bit you'd see. He's actually really nice.

Oh my God, there's the bell! Jeez, am I late or what? I'll see you at lunch, 'kay? Gotta run!"

She is gone. I lean against my locker, slightly out of breath. I can't believe she has agreed to go out with that ass again. I can't believe *her* — the clothes, the wild expression in her eyes, the stream of words flowing from her mouth. I am still leaning against my locker when the second bell rings, making me late for first class. Slowly I gather my books together, shut and lock my locker, and head down the hall.

* * *

The week slowly drifts by. I have a test for one class and an assignment due in another. Danelle bolts in and out of my days in strange costumes with even stranger conversations. I become more and more suspicious that she's using something.

Sunday morning I finally find a few minutes to go online for information about drug use. There are so many websites it's overwhelming, and they all list so many things associated with drug use. One site I find lists symptoms by the drug being used. Danelle has some of the symptoms — moodiness, not sleeping, excessive talking, hyperactivity, borrowing money, skipping school — but nothing that points to any one specific drug. I'm staring at the computer in a confused stupor when the phone rings.

"What are you doing?" Danelle demands, without even saying hello.

"Homework."

"Great, put it away and let's go to the mall. I have so-o-o much energy I can't stand it and I need company. I'll be over in ten minutes."

The phone is dead before I can speak. I stare at the receiver as the dead air surrounds me. Then the dial tone comes blasting through and I hang up. I wish I knew what was going on with her. Is it really drugs? And if it is, what exactly is she taking?

Danelle drives us to the mall. Today, instead of the gypsy skirt she wore most of last week with a variety of multi-coloured tops, she is wearing an old pair of sweat pants.

"What's with the pants?"

"PMS," she tells me. "Man, have I been bloated."

"There's a great herbal tea for that, apparently," I tell her, but she's not listening.

"You won't believe where Brian took me last night. He took me to this astounding club on Granville. He even had fake ID for me. Isn't that funny? I haven't used a fake ID for ages — everyone always tells me I look older than seventeen. The music was so totally cool," she continues, but I let my thoughts drift away.

I have never liked Brian and Danelle knows this. Usually she keeps her dates with him to herself, but today she is too "enraptured" by this club. I do tune in, however, when she stops talking about the date and starts telling me about what she did after he drove her home.

"I just borrowed my mother's car and drove to White Rock! It was so totally electrifying — really, Chris. I walked on the train tracks — a freight train came out of nowhere and I just managed to jump out of the way. And the ocean just seemed to go on and on forever…"

"Danelle, do you ever sleep?" She has found a parking spot for the car, but makes no move to get out.

"Sleep? I don't really need to. It's amazing, actually, but I have so much energy all the time and so many ideas! God, if you only knew half of them. I just think of stuff all the time. I have a great plan for doing schedules at school, but those old dinosaurs wouldn't listen when I tried to tell them on Friday. They just kept going on about the ensconced way of doing things and how maybe I should actually go to class and learn something. I got really pissed at that. I mean, here I have these outrageously awesome ideas on how to do things better and they can't be bothered to listen! I mean, wouldn't they like to be more productive? I just told them they were all a bunch of tight-asses and if they'd listen for ten minutes they'd see how good my ideas were. Then this one old cow of a secretary threatened to call the principal if I didn't leave. I think I'm going to get a tattoo. What do you think? I was thinking a little galaxy of stars on my shoulder, to go with our ceiling stars. I'm not too hot on needles but it's probably not that bad and you only live once."

"Danelle, I think you should see a doctor," I say

over her continuous flow of words. She stops talking and stares at me for a long second. "I'm serious. I think you should get checked out. Something is wrong. You don't sleep. You're doing dangerous things. You can't stop talking."

"There is nothing wrong with me, Christine." Surrounded by a black shadow, her eyes are unnaturally bright and darting and angry.

"There is! You aren't acting normal! God, Danelle, you climbed the roof of your house; you're walking railroads at midnight! You haven't slept in days. You don't make any sense when you talk. That isn't normal."

"Okay. So here is the term 'normal' as defined by Christine Dawson, one of the most pedestrian people I have ever met. Normal means getting eight and one-half hours of sleep every night. Normal means never trying anything new or daring to have an adventure. Normal is doing what every other person on the face of the earth is doing. Normal means never looking at things in a new way. Does that sound about right?" she asks, setting the parking brake.

"There is nothing wrong with doing new things, I never said there was!"

She snorts and shakes her head. "Please! You are terrified to try new things! You can't stand it that I am a free spirit. It drives you nuts that you can't contain me, fit me into a neat little package and understand me. Don't you dare paste your horrible labels on me and expect me to conform,

Christine, or we will not remain friends." She climbs out of the car and storms toward the doors of the mall. I carefully lock the car and follow her.

By the time I catch up with her, Danelle is no longer angry with me, and has, it seems, forgotten what we were talking about outside. At the food court, we each get a donut and a hot drink. The mall is crowded with people trying to escape the cold.

"Have you ever wondered if you could burgle a bank?" she whispers to me as we walk through the mall. I don't react. She must be joking, right? Burgle?

"Have you?" she repeats when I don't answer. I shake my head, determined not to encourage her. "I have. I think it could be done, you know, if you were smart about it. I bet the only reason people get caught is 'cause they aren't careful."

"You aren't thinking of trying it right now, are you?" I ask, ready to bolt.

"Hell, no. It takes tons of thought and planning," she informs me, cutting in front of me to go into a clothing store.

The store is crowded with girls our age, all taking advantage of the big post-Christmas sales. I haven't got any money, so I follow Danelle as she moves through the aisles, fingering sweaters and holding pants up against her. Eventually we end up at the back where belts and hosiery are displayed. By this time, Danelle has an armful of clothes, which she obviously intends to try on.

"How come there is never anyone around to help

you when you need it?" she asks loudly. I blush as several people turn to look at us. "Can you let me in a room, please?" she says, approaching an older woman wearing a nametag that says Candace.

Candace lets Danelle into a change room and I wait near the coats, wishing I had $300 to blow on a black suede jacket. Danelle bounces in and out of the change room about four times, wearing the most bizarre outfits in the store. At last she comes out carrying the clothes in a pile. She smiles brightly at Candace and dumps the stuff in her arms. "Thanks anyway."

We continue weaving our way through the crowds. Two stores down Danelle pauses, apparently interested in the display in the window.

"Come on, let's go in here. They have some really cool pants I want to look at," she says at last.

I follow her into the little boutique. It is much smaller than the other store and we are the only ones in it. The pants *are* nice. They have a low waist and flare out at the bottom. They even have a narrow black belt with a silver buckle.

"Should I try them on?" Danelle asks, holding them out in front of her, eyeing them critically.

"They're kind of expensive, aren't they?" I ask, showing her the price tag.

"That doesn't mean I can't try them on, does it?"

I shrug and turn to the next rack, flipping through the tops. Not having any money makes shopping kind of a bore, I decide.

Danelle comes out of the change room wearing

them. They look great on her, like she was born to wear them. I nod my approval.

"I don't think they fit," she decides, staring at herself in the mirror. "They feel a bit tight."

"They don't look tight."

"Well, they feel tight. Maybe it's the donut or something. I don't think I'll get them."

She disappears into the change room and emerges a few minutes later. "Thanks, but I'll have to pass this time," she says pleasantly as she hands the pants, neatly attached to their hanger, to the saleswoman.

"They looked really good, Danelle," I say as we walk away from the store.

"Yeah, Brian will love them."

My heart starts pounding when I realize what she has just said. She grins wickedly at me, pulling the elastic waist of her sweat pants out away from her body. I can just make out a black waistband before she snaps the elastic back over it.

"I can't believe you did that," I say, feeling my donut and hot chocolate rising in my throat. "What is wrong with you?"

"Nothing! That is such a rush! They won't miss their stupid old pants. They have insurance for that kind of thing."

"It doesn't matter, Danelle. It's still wrong. It's still stealing!"

"Oh, get a life, Christine!" she tells me, hands on hips, frowning. "You didn't do anything, so why are you freaking out?"

"You're insane," I tell her. "And I am going home." I ignore her calls to come back, and head for the bus stop. If she gets nailed for this, I don't want to be anywhere near her.

When I get home, my parents are having it out with Katie. Apparently she said she was going to be at her friend's place overnight but actually went to a rave downtown somewhere. She is sitting slumped on the couch, her hands holding her head — obviously hung over. I glance from her to my parents, who are absolutely purple with rage, and make a hasty retreat to my room.

When my parents are finished with her, Katie is like a caged animal, slamming around the house, cursing under her breath, kicking at furniture. She's been grounded as punishment, but I'm thinking she's not the only one getting punished. There's so much anger in our house I have trouble relaxing enough to fall asleep.

I have just managed to doze off when something starts tapping on my window. I jolt awake, really freaked out. I lie in bed staring at my softly glowing ceiling stars, terrified. There have been break-ins in the neighbourhood — kids looking for anything they can sell for drugs — and my imagination goes in to over-drive.

"Christine!" I immediately recognize Danelle's voice.

My heart stops pounding as I kneel on the bed and look out the window. Danelle is sitting on the fence with a handful of little rocks. When I open the window she stands up, rocking unsteadily on the narrow top of the fence.

"Come out with me! It is so beautiful out here. I want to go explore…" Her voice trails away as a car comes along the road, headlights becoming spotlights across Danelle's shadowy form. The illumination makes her white face seem even more ghost-like.

"You can't go exploring now! My God, Danelle, it's two in the morning," I tell her, speaking as softly as possible. "Go home, go to bed. Get some sleep."

"You are a lost cause, Christine," she says, but she climbs down reluctantly and in another second is gone.

* * *

I sleep poorly, only off and on the rest of the night, and wake up grouchy and tired. For the second morning in a row, Danelle isn't at our usual meeting place, and I make myself late for first class waiting for her. After last night's little drama I'm a little concerned, but not much — Danelle will show up eventually.

Jack finds me at my locker between first and second periods. I manage a smile for him, glad to see someone calm.

"Why are you flying around today?" he asks as I toss books left and right, looking for my writing journal.

I fill him in as we walk down the hall. When we arrive at the door of my writing class, I lean against the wall and close my eyes.

"Maybe you should talk to the counsellors about Danelle," Jack says.

"She'd freak if I did that. She thinks I'm too hung up on normal and should just leave her alone."

"Well, leave her alone then, if that's what she wants."

"Easy for you to say. She's going to hurt herself, Jack. Or get into serious trouble."

"Listen, Chris, you can't make her do anything. And if you push it and she stops talking to you, then what help will you be?" He is so damn logical sometimes. But I know he's right.

"So I just leave her alone, then?" I look up at Jack, who squeezes my shoulder gently.

"You're a great friend, Chris," he tells me. "Just stick close and let her know you're there for her."

"Hey, how did that family thing go with your dad and Jessica?" I ask, ready to change the subject.

"Oh, it was fine. Jessica and I behaved ourselves," he says, grinning at me cheekily. I realize how nice it is to have a normal conversation with someone. "Dad even let us have dessert."

"Big of him."

"Yeah, well, he's feeling pretty good about things, with Jessica being pregnant and everything."

"Is she huge?"

"She's pretty big. The baby's due in a month."

"How are you about it?" He wasn't impressed when his dad told him last fall.

"Resigned."

"I'll talk to you later, okay?" I say as the second bell rings. "Meet me for lunch."

He gives me a little salute and heads off to his art class. I duck into creative writing. It's going to be a long, long day.

Chapter 6

Danelle has disappeared. She never went home after calling me to the window Sunday night, and her parents haven't heard from her since. By Monday evening the Muellers have decided she's run away, possibly with Brian; his roommate hasn't seen him in days. They let the police know, but who knows how much help they'll be. Kids run away every single day and many don't want to be found. If Danelle's run away, there isn't much anyone can do.

Monday night I hardly sleep (again), imagining Danelle living as a runaway. Would she panhandle? Where would she sleep? I'm pretty protected from that world, but I read and watch enough TV to have an idea of what it's like. It's cold now, too. What is she thinking?

I spend most of Tuesday in a fog, trying desperately to think of where she might have gone, what she might be thinking. I rehash old conversations, going over and over things she's said lately, hoping for a clue. As the day wears on, I start to think of looking for her myself. I mention my idea to Jack at lunch, but he is less than supportive.

"She's off pulling some stunt to get attention, Chris," he says.

"You don't know that. She's been acting weird for over a week now. She's back with Brian again, which is not a good thing."

"I thought she ended things with him for good last time," he says, wiping mayonnaise from his mouth.

"Yeah, she did. But he called again last week. In fact, he's disappeared too, and I'm afraid they've gone off together. I'm afraid she's using something, Jack," I whisper, saying the words out loud for the first time.

He doesn't shoot me down or tell me I'm over-reacting, which in itself is frightening. It means he agrees with me. I sit silently, staring at my turkey sandwich.

"I'm going to look for her," I say finally. "Will you come with me?"

"I have a lot of work, Chris," he tells me, not making eye contact. "I can't afford to skip a whole day looking for Danelle. I'm sorry. I know you're worried about her, but…"

"But I'm not going to find her? But let the police do their jobs? But she'll come home when she's ready?" I fill in for him.

I know he doesn't get my friendship with Danelle.

And really, why should he? He thinks Danelle is a loon even on good days, and she gets a kick out of perpetuating that image.

But what Jack doesn't see is the Danelle who spends hours on the phone with me, bolstering my bruised ego when yet another guy I like turns out to be a loser or chooses someone else instead of me. Jack has never heard the little stories Danelle makes up for me where I actually get the guy and we walk off into the sunset together. Loony, I know, but it helps sometimes.

Jack has never heard Danelle talk about her acting, and he hasn't seen her perform. She's an amazing actress, becoming completely sub-merged in her character. She'll be great in the school play — she has the role of Frenchie in *Grease*. If she comes home, that is. If she isn't strung out somewhere with that jerk Brian. My fears about her using something are growing, especially since her parents found the stash of marijuana in her room.

By the end of the day I've decided to go by myself. I'm exhausted worrying about her, and I know I'll go crazy if I just sit around waiting for something to happen.

"Any word?" Jack asks, as I'm closing my locker after last period.

"No. I think I'm going to White Rock to look," I tell him as we leave the school together. "She took the car and drove down after a date with Brian, wandered the railroad ties."

"I'll take you," Jack says. "We can go right now if you want."

"Thanks," I say softly, not asking why he changed his mind. I'm just grateful he has.

* * *

The next morning I go into downtown Vancouver. Jack can't miss a whole day of school, but I'm determined to go, especially since our trip to White Rock was a complete bust. No one would even give us the time of day in those snooty shops and high-priced restaurants. We asked the few old men fishing from the pier, and walked along the long expanse of beach, stopping people and showing them Danelle's picture. But White Rock is a summer place and it was pretty dead on a winter afternoon.

I'm more hopeful about Granville Street. It's known as a hang out for street kids, runaways, just about anyone with nowhere else to go. I start at the upscale end — Holt Renfrew, the old Birks building which is now a London Drugs, Pacific Centre Mall, glitzy little boutiques and old heritage buildings with offices in them. There are lots of business people rushing along with cell phones and briefcases at this time of day.

I walk quickly, my hands deep in my pockets, as it's really cold this morning. As I walk, I keep scanning, watching for that familiar face, listening for that familiar laugh. I have Danelle's picture with me, tucked in my coat pocket, and I've even brought handfuls of loose change (from Katie's coin jar) just in case.

The sun gets higher in the sky and the air warms a little. I buy a hot chocolate and sip it as I walk along. The smell of chocolate is comforting. Granville gets busier as the morning goes on, and people bump into me, brush past, mutter at me to get out of the way.

I'm done with the upscale end of Granville, with its fancy boutiques and little bistros. At this end of the street are "adult entertainment" shops alternating with pawnshops. I pass a seedy looking hotel. Through windows across the front I see shelves of towels and sheets with a price list mounted on the wall: *Rooms by the hour*. At the corner of Davie and Granville, two men who are unsteady on their feet are having an argument, and their voices rise above the sounds of the traffic and the music coming from a CD shop. I skirt around them carefully, trying not to inhale as I pass.

Every so often I stop to ask someone who looks like they've been down here a while if they've seen Danelle. "Have you seen this girl?" "Do you recognize this girl?" "Have you ever seen anyone who looks like this?" "Does she look familiar?" The questions begin to run together as I ask them over and over and over, holding out my little snapshot, waiting patiently to be told no, no, no, nononononononono.

At lunch I stop and buy a hamburger. Two old guys watch me as I leave the counter. They have stubbled cheeks and rags around their hands. The smell of them overpowers the greasy beef smell of my lunch, and I hurry back outside, away from their eyes. I am ashamed of myself, knowing Danelle would have asked if they were hungry, given them money. I am not that brave.

I eat as I walk, tired and close to giving up. Why am I bothering? Danelle's not here. I've been walking around for hours and no one has recognized her photo. I rub my hand across my eyes and choke back the sob that rises in my throat. I have pretty much decided to catch the bus and go home, when I see yet another little group of kids standing around a bus stop.

"I was wondering if you might have seen this girl?" I ask, showing them the picture. It's getting filmy from my fingerprints, but the image is still true. One by one they shake their heads. Some don't even bother looking at it.

The last kid, a boy not much older than Katie, holds on to it for a long time, staring at me, not the picture. He is wearing a knit toque and layers of jackets and sweaters. His hands are red and chapped, the fingernails bitten down to almost nothing. His icy blue stare makes me nervous and I start to fidget. I wait, trying not to stare at the baseball-sized hole in his jeans that is exposing his underwear.

"She's pretty," he says at last, and I flinch.

His voice hasn't even changed yet — he's nothing but a baby. What's he doing down here?

"Isn't she pretty, Steve?" he asks, shoving the

photo into his friend's face. Steve doesn't look overly impressed. "Yeah, well, you're a homo anyway," he mutters when Steve doesn't respond. "I'd take her."

The others laugh at this and a bit of jostling goes on, with Toque Boy still holding my photo. "She give out?" he asks me, frowning from under seriously bushy eyebrows.

My heart is pounding. I have no idea how to deal with this. I look away and spot another cluster of kids leaning against a nearby building. One of the kids, a dark-haired girl about my age, is wearing a long gray trench coat that is surprisingly clean for the neighbourhood. Her face is partially hidden by a baseball cap, but her mouth looks oddly familiar. I grab my photo from Toque Boy and move toward the girl, a strange feeling gripping me

"Danelle?" I call, almost crying as I get close. She looks at me and takes off, running as hard as she can. I take off after her, pounding down the sidewalk faster than I have ever run in my life. I am sure it is Danelle. Why else would she take off like that?

"Danelle! Wait! Please! Wait! Talk to me!" I scream as I run, oblivious to the strange looks from the people I fly past. I just see her duck into a building. The locked door swings into place with a click before I can grab it.

I bang on the glass with my fists, tears leaving wet paths down my cheeks. "Danelle! For God's sake, talk to me!" I cry, but the building has swallowed her.

"Hey," a voice says from behind me. I turn,

defeated and exhausted. A girl who is covered in rings — nose, ear, lip, tongue, eyebrow — is watching me, curious. "You okay?" I nod, slumping down onto the step.

"That girl you were chasing," the girl says, sitting down beside me, "what were you calling her?"

"Danelle," I say through my fingers. "Her name is Danelle." I sit up suddenly, my brain taking over again. "You know her. Is she staying here? Could you get her to come down and talk to me?"

"Hey, hold on." The girl holds up a hand, revealing a small inventory of rings on her fingers. "I don't know where she lives, but it isn't here. Maybe her pimp lives here. And her name isn't Danielle."

Pimp! There's no way Danelle is hooking, but I struggle to stay polite. I have to get information.

"Danelle," I correct her.

"Don't matter. She doesn't live here and her name's not Danelle. She's been working down here for months, hiding out from her stepmother or something."

Months. Danelle's been missing for days. Three of them. It isn't her. I don't know whether to be relieved or sorry.

"Thank you for your help," I say softly, standing up. The gray eyes that follow me are hollow and huge in the little face. "If I offered you something to go buy dinner, would you be offended?" I ask. She shakes her head and gladly accepts the coins I drop into her hand.

Chapter 7

I fall asleep on the bus on the way home and wake up just before my stop. It has started to rain and, by the time I get in the dry, welcoming house, I'm pretty wet. I think of all the kids I met out on the cold, wet pavement of Granville Street, and I hope that wherever Danelle is, she's at least inside right now.

Katie is in the kitchen making supper. Our parents haven't come home yet, thankfully — they won't be thrilled about where I spent my day.

"There was a call for you," my sister tells me. She is standing at the stove, stirring something that smells wonderful. "Mrs. Mueller. Some guy named Brian called them. He doesn't know where Danelle is, hasn't seen her since Saturday."

"Damn," I mutter under my breath as I collapse into a chair. "Thanks, Katie."

"Who's Brian?"

"Danelle's boyfriend. We thought they might have taken off together, but I guess not."

"Did you really go down to Granville by your-self looking for her?" I hear admiration in my sister's voice. I nod. "Holy. I guess you didn't find her, huh?"

"No. I'm going to have a quick shower and get warm. When's dinner ready?"

"About half an hour. Mom and Dad had an appointment. They'll be late." I nod again and head for the stairs. "Christine?"

"Yeah?" I stop. If she makes a crack about Danelle, I'll pound her, I really will.

"I just wanted to say I hope she's okay. Danelle, I mean. I hope they find her or she comes home. That's all."

We look at each other for several long seconds and I feel the prickle of tears behind my eyelids. I blink and smile wearily at her. "Thanks, Katie. I appreciate that."

She nods and goes back to the pot on the stove. I continue upstairs to my shower.

* * *

"Christine, will you stay after class today?" Ms. Armstrong asks the next morning.

I spend the rest of writing class fretting about what she wants. It's either to give me hell for skip-ping, or to give me back the story I gave her to read a few weeks ago. Either way, I'm a bundle of nerves by the time the bell rings for break. The room slowly empties and we are alone.

Ms. Armstrong invites me to sit. She leans forward, elbows on her desk, hands clasped. She has a very earnest way about her when she is being particularly serious.

"First let me say I'm sorry I've kept your work so long. I have no really good excuse. But I'll tell you right now, Christine, get used to it! Publishers are notorious for keeping things forever. You'll wonder if they ever got it. Anyway. That isn't why I called you in." She smiles.

I relax slightly. She doesn't care that I wasn't here yesterday. My story is on the desk in front of her. She smoothes the small stack of papers with her hands, staring at the words written on the first page.

"This is good." The room rings with those three little words. She can have no idea how hard it was for me to share it with her. "It is still quite rough, but you probably know that. A piece of work goes through so many edits and rewrites before it is in its final form. Don't worry about that. Don't ever worry about polishing. Getting a first draft down is often the hard part. But the editing and rethinking and reworking, that is where the real rewards are." She looks up at me, her eyes blue behind her glasses. I am hanging on every word she says, but I can't quite stop hearing "This is good."

"Now, what I am proposing to you is that we work this through together. I would like to see you polish it by the end of the term. Then we'll figure out what to do about finding a magazine that will take it, although there are no guarantees."

"You think someone would publish it?" I ask, my mouth hanging open.

"Possibly. As I said, there are no guarantees about anything. But first — lots of polishing, tightening, editing. Think you're up to the challenge?" Ms. Armstrong is smiling at me again. She picks up the story and hands it to me, rising as she does.

"Definitely. I never even thought that far. I always just wrote because I wanted to. I've never shown my stuff to anyone before," I confess, hugging the precious pages to my chest.

"Well, then, I'm glad you took a chance and trusted me. I'm enjoying your work in class, Christine. You have promise. So keep taking the risk of rejection and one day, you won't be rejected."

She walks me to the door of the class, and I think I say good-bye before drifting off down the hall to my locker. I'm pretty sure my feet never once hit the floor. I can't wait to tell Danelle — she'll be thrilled. And then I remember that she has disappeared, that no one knows where she's gone or if she'll be back, and my good feeling fades.

* * *

Friday, Jack gives me a ride home. It's been a long, hellish week and there is still no word from Danelle. I dread the phone ringing — the Muellers have been phoning daily wondering if I've heard from her. Like I wouldn't phone them immediately if I did! And every ring could be the news that Danelle's cold, dead body has been found...

My worry and fear for Danelle are slowly being replaced by a red-hot anger. I keep asking myself how she can just disappear without a word to anyone and not think for a second that people are worrying about her, that people are afraid she's dead or in trouble.

My mother's car isn't in the driveway when Jack and I pull up, but I can tell as soon as I open the door that Katie is home. She has her stereo blaring and her junk is littering the front hallway. Jack and I have to step over her backpack, her jacket, her shoes, a bag with dance stuff spilling out of it, and a stack of library books.

"Katie, get down here and clean up this crap before someone kills themselves tripping on it," I yell up the stairs. Something rude drifts back down to me. I turn to Jack. "Did I tell you she went to a rave last weekend with some friends? She came home pretty drunk."

"How'd you find that out?" Jack asks, sliding onto a chair in the kitchen.

I pull out glasses and plates and raid the fridge for something to eat. "Her friend's brother thought Mom was someone else when she called, and told her where they were. You should have heard the fireworks. Has it been that long since I talked to you?"

"You've had other things on your mind," he

reminds me. He scarfs down the sandwich I put in front of him in what seems like two bites. "I don't remember you telling me. Maybe I should have a talk with the girl."

"Not funny."

"Your sister is a real case, isn't she?"

"She was pretty sick, let me tell you. She had Mom and Dad up half the night looking after her. And then they made her go to my grandparents' for dinner on Sunday."

"Ah, the oldest punishment in the book," Jack says, nodding his head wisely. "I think my mom did something similar to me the first time I got drunk."

"Which was?"

"About two weeks after Dad moved out."

"I didn't know that," I say quietly. "Why didn't you tell me?"

Jack shrugs and clears his throat. "Why? It was embarrassing and stupid. Anyway, what are your parents going to do?" Jack picks up the uneaten half of my sandwich and wolfs it down.

"Actually, they grounded her. She just doesn't seem to care about anything these days. Except her friends and boys and what she can do to piss people off. She got an interim report from her algebra teacher last week and Dad nearly hit the roof."

"Stop talking about me behind my back," Katie says, appearing suddenly in the doorway.

She scowls at me, then turns a charming smile on Jack. My eyebrows rise. She's wearing one of

Dad's shirts (the kid never wears her own stuff) and one of her several pairs of jeans with torn knees. She must have showered after school because her face is clean and young-looking, and her hair is considerably less freakish than usual.

"Hey, Katie," Jack says, raising his second sandwich in tribute. "Hear you went on a bit of a bender."

"My sister should mind her own business," Katie tells him, snarling at me before turning her radiant smile back to Jack. "It was no big deal," she says, playing with a damp curl. "I mean, everyone got way over-emotional about it."

"Next time, bribe your friends to be quiet," Jack says, winking at her. Katie turns fifteen shades of pink and is momentarily speechless.

"I'll try to remember that," she finally whispers and disappears back upstairs.

I can't believe what I've just seen. My little sister was *flirting* with Jack! I want to laugh, but at the same time I'm pissed off. What the hell does she think she's doing? She looked like a fool. I glance at Jack, wondering what he's thinking, but he's busy polishing off the rest of the food. He probably didn't even notice.

* * *

Next night the phone rings.

"Hello?"

"I'm home!" says a familiar voice. "And I—"

"Danelle!"

"The bus just got in this second and I was the first one off to call my best friend in the whole world. I told the woman I was sitting beside that you would come and pick me up because you missed me and would want to hear all about my adventures. I told her about the Space Needle and the market and the malls!"

"Where the hell have you been?"

"Holy, wait till you see all the impedimenta I got! But this woman from the bus, she's got two grandchildren, a boy named Aaron and a girl named Kylie, and they live in Edmonton. She was going to Edmonton after visiting her sister in Vancouver for a few days. Her husband works for some big firm in Seattle. She likes Seattle but misses her family."

"Are you okay? We've been worried…"

"I didn't miss my family! Holy, it was nice to not have anyone yelling or nagging or spying on me. I'm sure glad it isn't raining 'cause I'd be soaked by now! It was raining when we left Seattle. Did I tell you how I got down there? Funny story. I was planning to go downtown and hit some clubs—"

"What is wrong with you? You just disappeared."

"Will you come and get me? Please? I need a ride home and then I can tell you all about my exploits."

Whatever Danelle's taking, she's definitely high on it now. How would I be helping her by rushing downtown to get her? I don't even have a car — my parents are out for the night.

"I can't, Danelle," I say. "But I'll call your parents and—"

But Danelle has hung up.

* * *

I spend most of Sunday sitting at the desk in my room, making doodles in my notebooks. I have so much homework, but at the moment I don't care. Everything feels like it's bearing down on me — schoolwork, Danelle's problems, the end of the school year, the part-time job I'm supposed to be hunting for.

I hear the doorbell ring downstairs and reluctantly get up to answer it. It's Danelle. For a second I toy with the idea of shutting the door in her face, but I can tell by looking at her that something's changed.

"I screwed up," she says, "and I'm sorry. I'm sorry I worried you and my parents and everyone. I'm sorry you skipped school to look for me. I wasn't thinking clearly." She's waiting for me to respond but I don't know what to say. I'm still so angry.

"But I'm fine now. You have to believe me, Chris," she pleads, reaching for my hand, which is still holding the door. "Please believe me when I say I'm fine now. I had a long talk with my mother and father. I promise to see a counsellor at school first thing tomorrow, okay? But I'm fine now. I need you. You're my best friend and I miss you."

I don't want to give in to her. It is so easy for her to say these words, to look so repentant. She's an actress for God's sake! But I can feel the change in her, hear it in her voice, and see it in her eyes. The hunted, wild look is gone and I can tell she's had some sleep. She is calm and patient, not bouncing all over the place. I relax, but only slightly.

"You have to see a counsellor, Danelle," I tell her firmly. "The way you were acting, that's just not normal. Even for someone who doesn't do normal."

"I know. You're right. But you won't let last week invalidate our whole friendship will you?"

"Don't ever, ever, do that again. Not ever," I say softly, pulling my hand away. "Do you understand? Because I can't handle it again."

"Yeah. I know." She leans over and hugs me. I finally let myself forgive her, and hug her back. "Can I come in? It's kind of cold out here," she says. I stand back and let her through the door.

Chapter 8

"Hey, Chris," Jack says, appearing at my locker at two-forty on a Friday afternoon just before Valentine's Day.

"Hey, yourself."

"You going home?" he asks, falling into step beside me as I head down the hall.

"Straight. I have tons of homework to do this weekend."

We push through the heavy, orange fire doors. It's cold today — the kind of cold that gets inside you and doesn't let you warm up. The last couple of weeks since Danelle's "adventure" have been pretty slow and uneventful — a nice change, to be honest.

"I guess you won't have time to drive out to Cloverdale with me on Saturday, then," Jack says, kicking at a pop can on the sidewalk. He has his hands shoved deep in the pockets of his jeans. His backpack thumps against his back as he walks.

"Why do I want to go to Cloverdale?"

"Well," he says, then clears his throat. "It seems I'm a brother again. Another sister."

"Jessica had the baby?"

"Yeah. A few days ago."

"How are you?"

"I'm neutral."

I know he's fibbing because he's all slouched over and gangly, as though his body is too heavy to hold up, typical of Jack when he's feeling weighed down with stuff.

"I have to go out and see her and the baby, though. Right away. If I don't, I'm going to be forever branded as a jerk. I have enough problems with Jessica without adding that. But I don't want to go alone."

"When do you want to go?"

"We could go whenever you want. I just have to let them know when we're coming."

"Okay. Well, if it's okay with your dad and Jessica, why don't we go after dinner?" I suggest. "That'll give me most of the day to work on stuff. Maybe around seven? Would that work? It only takes about half an hour to get there, doesn't it?"

"Forty-five minutes, actually. I'll check and get back to you, okay?"

* * *

Jack picks me up Saturday just after dinner in his mom's car, which is a nice treat. It's clean and it doesn't break down.

"So, what are your dad and Jessica naming the baby?" I ask, turning to look at him. I can tell he put some effort into his appearance — he's wearing his best frayed jeans and black leather jacket — and am impressed by how hard he is trying to get along with his stepmother.

"Angela Lynn."

"That's a nice name. Angela. Is it for someone, a grandmother or something?"

"I think the Angela is for Jessica's mom. Thanks for coming, Chris," Jack says, throwing me a quick smile.

Mr. Burrows answers the door when Jack knocks. "Jess," Mr. Burrows calls as we come down the hall, "the kids are here."

Jessica is nursing baby Angela in a rocking chair, a large pillow supporting the baby in her lap. I feel Jack stiffen beside me. He takes two steps back and ends up almost behind me. He has no idea where to put his eyes.

"This is my friend, Christine. Chris, this is Jessica," he mumbles, remembering his manners.

Mr. Burrows shakes my hand and then shakes Jack's. I have met him only once before and that was years ago. He and Jack look a lot alike, aside from the hair. Mr. Burrows doesn't have much.

"And this is Angela Lynn," he says proudly, standing beside his wife. He's all puffed up like one of the peacocks in Stanley Park, and a massive grin is threatening to break his jaw.

"Congratulations," I say, smiling.

When Angela finishes nursing, Jessica quickly snaps her shirt closed and straightens herself out. Within a second, you'd never know what has been going on.

Jack relaxes and moves into the room. He goes over to Jessica and says something low that I don't catch. He strokes Angela's little clenched fist and then we all sit down.

Jack, sitting beside me on the couch, doesn't completely relax the entire time we're there. He and Jessica seldom speak directly to each other. He talks to his dad about school and his art and his chances at the scholarship he is working for. Jessica and I talk baby. After about half an hour, Jack clears his throat and stands up.

"I guess we should get going home, eh, Chris?" he says, holding his hand out to me. I take it and let him pull me up. He doesn't let go of my hand as we all move down the narrow hall to the front door.

"It was very nice of you to come," Jessica says. She glances at our clasped hands and smiles a knowing smile at me. What has Jack said about us? Surely they know we are only friends. "I hope we'll be able to count on you for babysitting sometimes, Jack," she teases.

"Yeah, sure. Whenever," he says as we head down the stairs.

"It was nice meeting you," I call. "Congratulations again on the baby." They wave as we climb in the car and drive away.

"Sorry I dragged you all the way out here," he says. "But thanks for coming with me. It was easier, you know, than being by myself."

"That's okay. I know it's tough seeing them together, especially now with a baby. It'll get easier, though," I say, not at all sure that it will. "I think Jessica thought we were dating."

"Does it bother you if she does?" he asks, rather roughly.

"No. I mean we were holding hands," I tell him, wondering vaguely why the thought bothers him so much.

"What did you think of my half sister?" he asks at last. "Does she pass as far as babies go?"

"She was cute, I guess. She's only a few days old. Give her a few months and then she'll be interesting."

"I somehow doubt that."

We drive for several miles in silence. I can tell Jack is stewing about something by the way he's holding the steering wheel in a death grip and glaring at the road. I watch the fields and farmhouses slip past as we drive through the darkened countryside. Finally he speaks.

"Carina's been all excited about meeting her new sister, but when she finally got to see her yesterday Dad wouldn't let her hold her or even touch her. God, the guy's a prick! Carina cried for hours. And he's been cancelling our weekends for the past month so they can 'get ready for the baby.' He doesn't care about *us* anymore."

I reach over and squeeze his arm, but he just shakes his head.

"Maybe things will get better in a few weeks when Angela isn't so new anymore," I suggest, dropping my hand.

"She isn't a new toy, Chris," Jack tells me, his voice a little sad. "Whatever. It isn't like I didn't expect it."

There is nothing I can say to that, so I say nothing.

Chapter 9

"I can't believe it's almost March," Alana says, throwing her pencil down on the dining room table.

She leans back in her chair, fanning her thick, black hair out behind her. I love Alana's hair. It's extremely straight and shiny as polished ebony. She says she'd like to have waves and curls like I have, but try getting waves and curls to behave. With her almond-shaped eyes and creamy skin, she's gorgeous. I keep telling her she should be a model. As partners for a couple of geography projects this semester, she and I have become pretty good friends.

"Thank God, is all I can say," I mutter, struggling to label a small map of British Columbia. Our geography project is driving us both crazy, but thankfully we are almost finished. I glance at my watch.

"Are you hungry? Want to stop for something to eat?" I ask, my own stomach grumbling.

"Sounds great," she says, following me into the kitchen.

She takes a seat at the kitchen table while I rummage through cupboards and the fridge.

"So, did you hear from UBC yet?" Alana asks, trying not to laugh as I struggle to cut bagels without chopping off my fingers.

"Yeah, last week. I got in," I tell her. It is definitely possible to be absolutely thrilled about something and at the same time be terrified beyond measure.

"That's so awesome, Chris! Good for you. You're going to be a great writer."

"I haven't decided to accept, Alana," I tell her. "I'm still thinking about it."

"Why'd you apply if you weren't going to accept?"

"The writing program seemed like a good idea at the time," I tell her, truthfully. I shrug and don't finish. Alana nods and I'm glad to not have to explain any further. "Have you heard from any of the schools you applied to?" I ask. I hold our glasses under the ice machine in the fridge and miss the first part of her answer in the thunder of falling cubes.

"… haven't decided where to go. I thought, before, that I'd like to go away from home but now…" She stops speaking and blushes.

"But now?" I set a plate and a glass of pop in front of her and sit down. Alana stares at the food, still red in the face.

"There's this guy…"

"A guy? How come you never said anything! How long have you been going out?"

"Well, that's the thing. We're not going out. I don't even know if he likes me, really."

"Who is he?"

"His name is Cole. He plays soccer with my brother Mike. I see him at games a lot. We've talked and stuff. But that's all. He's never acted like he cares. So I don't know what to do."

"You're thinking that if he asks you out, you want to stay here and see what happens, but if he doesn't, you want to run away, right?" I take a guess, teasing her a bit.

"Something like that," Alana agrees, finally picking up a sandwich half. "My parents are really on my case to decide about going."

"Want me to talk to Cole?" I offer.

"NO! Chris, don't, please."

I reach behind me, grab a couple of napkins from the shelf, and hand one to Alana. "I won't, don't worry. I'm just teasing."

"Okay, good. Don't tell anyone, will you? Not even Danelle?"

I promise, still amazed that quiet Alana has a crush. This guy would be crazy not to ask her out. She's the nicest person I know.

The phone rings as we're organizing material half an hour later. It's Danelle.

"What's up?" I ask, frowning at a page of notes that make no sense. No title on the top of the page, no references to books. I shove it at Alana, who takes it and reads it.

"I just wanted to say hi," Danelle says, her voice a whisper.

"Well, hi to you too. I'm kind of busy right now, Danelle. Can I talk to you later? Alana and I are in the middle of this stupid report."

"Oh. Well, I didn't mean to interrupt or anything. I was just, you know, kind of alone."

"Can you speak up a bit, Danelle? I can't hear you."

"I said I was just kind of, by myself. So I thought I'd call and talk to you," she says, her voice only slightly louder than before.

I frown. What is it now? *Why* now? "Can I call you back, Danelle?"

"Oh. Okay, sure. Sorry to be a bother…" Danelle's voice trails off and she hangs up the phone.

* * *

The rest of the weekend is insane: homework, a huge fight with Katie over a ripped shirt, dinner at my grandparents', and another two-hour stint on the geography project (which, for the amount of time it's taking us, should be worth more than twenty-five per cent of our grade). Consequently I don't get back to Danelle.

In fact I don't even think of her again until Monday morning when I open my locker and a small piece of notebook paper falls out. It is folded so tightly it takes me several seconds just to open it. I recognize Danelle's handwriting right away; it's the size of the print that baffles me. And the words she has written:

Dear Chris, Sorry I'm such a bother all the time. I know you would rather spend time with Alana than me. I just have to get used to the idea, I guess. D

I read it through three times, flipping it over to see if there is more on the other side. Nothing. When did she write this? She was fine Friday when we said good-bye. Then I remember that I didn't return her call.

I arrive at my locker after last class to find her sitting on the floor, waiting for me. She glances up at me through her bangs. She looks tired.

"Hi," I say, spinning the dial on my lock. "Where've you been all day?"

"I've been here," she says softly.

"What's with the note? Are you auditioning for a new role or something?" I ask, squatting down beside her on the litter-strewn floor.

Danelle picks at her left forefinger, peeling skin away from the cuticle until little droplets of blood pop out. Then she puts it in her mouth. I want to slap her hand away, but I just turn my eyes, feeling slightly ill. Around us, swarms of kids push past, laden with packs of books. Their voices are loud and insistent, and twice I'm kicked and growled at.

"I tried to call you a bunch of times, but your sister kept saying you were out," she says through her finger. She takes it out of her mouth but doesn't start picking at it again, thank God. "You never called back or anything."

"I'm sorry I didn't get back to you Saturday, but you wouldn't believe how busy the whole weekend was."

She looks sad and forgotten, sitting there on the dirty floor. But instead of sympathy I feel anger, mostly at my darling sister for not giving me my messages, but also at Danelle. What is with all the melodrama? Usually she'd just blast me to my face for not calling her back. This sad-sack routine is new.

"Come on, Danelle, you know my stupid sister! She never told me you called. You know she's a brat! I worked all Saturday and Sunday with Alana, I was out Saturday night, and we were at my grandparents' yesterday. Okay?"

Someone's portable stereo catches me in the shoulder as it passes and I fall forward, barely catching myself before I land on Danelle.

"Watch it, jerk!" I yell, but whoever it was is long gone.

"I guess I forgot about how Katie is," Danelle says slowly.

"Danelle," I say as we stand up, "are you okay now? No more of those notes?"

"Yeah, I'm good," she says and starts picking at her finger again.

Chapter 10

The second and third notes arrive at the end of that week. Just like the first they are folded into tiny squares, are printed in tiny writing, and are so strange:

Dear Chris, I'm trying to study for this test in French but I don't understand the stuff. Why do they make me learn stuff I don't understand? D Later: I think I failed that test. No, I know I failed that test. I used to love French, too. It's so musical, so poetic. Not like English. D

Dear Chris, I am sitting here in history trying to concentrate. I watch Mr. Singh's lips move but nothing he says makes any sense. Nothing makes any sense these days. I feel like I'm in some kind of a cloud or something. I can hear your voice, though, clear and clean, wrenching me from my doom. D

At the end of the day Danelle and I walk home together. I have tucked the notes in my pocket and pull them out, showing them to her.

"What's with the tiny printing?" I ask. "I think I need glasses — I can hardly read it."

"Sorry," she whispers in this new breathless voice she has taken on.

"Sorry I need glasses?" I tease and bump against her, but she doesn't smile. "Didn't you have some kind of drama thing this afternoon?"

She doesn't answer, and after a few more failed attempts at conversation I just concentrate on walking, my mind on a troublesome bit of the story I've been working on all week. The characters won't behave and I have a looming deadline. I never realized that characters actually control a story; I always thought the writer did. But try and get a character to do something they don't want to, and you just end up with a problem.

It's warm this afternoon and I can smell spring. I notice crocuses in several gardens, and the old guy at the end of the street the school is on has moved his relic of a collector's car out of the garage into the driveway and put up the makeshift canopy cover he uses in good weather.

"Mr. Davis is feeling optimistic," I say, pointing to the black gangster car.

Danelle doesn't answer. We arrive at the corner where we normally go our separate ways. Danelle lights her third cigarette and I notice for the first time that some of her other fingers are torn. The raw redness on top of the nicotine-yellow stains is gruesome. What is with that habit? Isn't smoking gross enough for her?

"Did you want to come over?" I ask, staring at a spot above her right shoulder. I'm beginning to wonder if she's coming down with something. She's never this quiet.

"Over?" she repeats. "You mean to your house?" She looks at me blankly.

"Yes."

"I don't know. Should I?" she asks, obviously confused by the question. "I think I'm supposed to go straight home. Isn't there something I was supposed to do?"

I take a breath and let it out slowly. "I know you were supposed to go to rehearsal this afternoon. Is everything okay, Danelle? You're acting really weird."

"I am? I'm sorry. I'm tired, although I'm sleeping tons, and I had a big fight with Brian and stuff."

"Do you want to come over to my house so we can talk?" I ask again.

"Will you come to mine? Is that okay? I don't think I have the energy to walk all the way to your place." She is already moving down her street before I answer.

Upstairs in her bedroom Danelle immediately curls up in the corner on her bed, her legs folded, her arms wrapped around her knees. No music, no candles, no incense. I frown, but take up my usual place on the cushions on the floor by the window.

It's dark in her room; she hasn't opened the blinds or turned on the light. Her galaxy shimmers faintly above us.

"What happened with Brian?"

"The other night we were, you know, fooling around, doing stuff at his place, and all of a sudden he's all over me and he wouldn't get off. I kept pushing at him, telling him not to, telling him I didn't want that, but he wouldn't listen," she says, her voice flat, her eyes not meeting mine.

"He didn't…he didn't force you, did he?"

"No! No, he stopped eventually, before anything … you know, before. But it scared me," she says, her eyes growing larger, shimmering with tears.

I crawl over to the bed and sit beside her, hug her. "It's okay, Danelle, really. Everything is okay. He stopped, didn't he? Did you leave then? Right away, just come home?"

"He keeps pushing, you know?" she says without answering my questions. "Says if I loved him I wouldn't be so stubborn. He tells me he could have any girl he wants. What am I going to do?"

Danelle pushes away from me, rubbing at her damp face. She tucks her hair behind her ears and shakes her head at me. "I should break up with him, shouldn't I," she says. "I don't want to stop seeing him. I like him a lot. I just wish he'd stop bugging me about sex. I don't want to, not yet."

"We could get you a chastity belt," I suggest. I have only a vague idea what one is, but Danelle laughs and I relax.

* * *

"You're nuts," Jack tells me. The waitress, a tiny Chinese woman, bows at us and puts plates of food on the table between us. This little Chinese restaurant, just blocks from school, is a popular place — it's always busy.

"I'm not nuts, I'm just not sure." I shrug and sip my green tea. "Besides, what does it matter to you if I go to university or not?"

I have to let the admissions people at UBC know whether I'll be taking the spot they offered me in the writing program, but I keep putting it off. What if I don't measure up to the rest of the class?

"Chris, you love to write and you are good at it. They want you in the program. Go for it! What's the worst that could happen?"

"I could be no good."

"I doubt you'll find that out in the first couple of weeks," Jack says, shaking his head at me. "And isn't that why we go to school? If you were really that awful they wouldn't have accepted you in the first place, for one thing. And for another, you'll learn stuff and get better."

How do you argue with that? I bite my lip, chewing on the self-doubt and anxiety churning inside me. At the same time, the other voice inside me tells me how wonderful it would be to sit in a room with other writers and talk about writing as much as I want. It's very confusing.

"Has Danelle been filling your head with crap again?" Jack asks, unzipping his polar vest.

"No, she hasn't said anything."

How could she? I hardly see her, mostly because she is skipping school a lot, but also because I've been really busy. Most of our interaction comes from the little notes she continues to stuff in my locker. I have quite a collection:

Hi. I'm just sitting outside having a smoke. I know, I know, I should quit. But I'm not strong enough to quit. I'm pathetic, really. I don't know why you bother with me at all. Why do you? D

I can't concentrate today. I told Mr. Archer I wasn't feeling well and skipped out of class. I'm such a lousy actress. I'll never make it on the stage. I can't remember my lines, can't sing. I'm so useless. D

I can't sit still, Chris. My legs twitch and my eyebrows twitch. I'm sure I have some deadly disease. Is there anything of mine you particularly want? I would like you to take care of my things for me, okay? When I die? Promise me. You're my best, best friend in the whole world and you're the only one who understands me at all. D

I'm out of smokes. I can't believe I ran out of

*smokes and I'm flat broke. I know I should
quit. I can hear your voice telling me to quit.
Have you got the pictures of diseased lungs
ready to show me? I'm so tired, Chris. But I
sleep all the time. I know I'm boring you. I'm
sorry. I'm fine, just a low self-image day. D*

"Are you still getting those notes?" Jack asks,
peering at me over his cup of green tea.

"Yeah. She's obviously unhappy about something but she won't tell me what the problem is.
She keeps saying she doesn't know. Or she says
she's just having a down time and everyone is
entitled to that." I shrug and take a big bite of
chow mein.

"Well, she could be right. I mean, we do all get
down sometimes and grad is coming up. Maybe
she's starting to realize she may not graduate if
she doesn't actually do some of the work," he
says.

"I'm not so sure that's it, Jack. I mean Danelle
has never cared about her grades, or whether she
passes or fails her classes. Why all of a sudden?"

"Don't know," he says with a shrug, and picks
up an egg roll with his chopsticks.

"Actually," I say slowly, picking my words
carefully, "I'm beginning to think she's depressed,
not just down."

"Really, depressed?" Jack says when he is finished chewing.

"I don't know. None of her behaviour makes any

sense to me. First she's flying off the walls and disappearing, and now she's talking about being useless and a failure. I don't know, but I'm worried."

Jack doesn't say anything and, really, what can he say? I pick up my chopsticks and wrestle with an egg roll. This place is not the prettiest, with its plastic flower arrangements and paper menus, and I wouldn't use the rest room on a bet, but the food is good. When we're done Jack pays the bill and we head outside.

"I am so glad it's Friday," I say as I buckle my seat belt. "Although I don't know why. I have so much homework I can hardly carry my backpack. It seems like the closer we get to the end of the school year, the worse the teachers get about work."

"Tell me about it. I have two shifts this weekend, a paper is due next week, and Dad wants to take us all out for dinner on Sunday for Jessica's birthday." Jack navigates the parking lot and gets out onto the street.

"It's great that he's finally seeing you guys again," I say. Jack grunts, but his nod makes me think he's glad too.

I lean back in the seat and close my eyes. When Jack's car works, it's actually not a bad way to get around. He has sheepskin seat covers and an awesome stereo system, and he keeps his car cleaner than he keeps his bedroom, so that's a plus.

Chapter 11

"I'm worried about my friend," I say, nervously picking at a hangnail.

The image of Danelle's torn, bloody fingers pops into my head and I stop. Shoving my hands between my knees, I stare at the top of the counsellor's desk instead. It is covered with papers and books with titles like *The Teenage Mind* and *Helping the Troubled Teen*. Danelle would be in convulsions reading those titles if she was here. But she's not. I am.

I've spoken to the counsellor — the same one we've had since arriving at the school almost five years ago — exactly once. I know her name is Ms. Yu and she's still in her twenties. She's nice enough, but I doubt she'll be able to help. This was Jack's idea.

"What's happening with your friend?" she asks.

"She's been really down for a couple of weeks. I think she's depressed but she won't admit it. She keeps saying it's just a low time, no big deal."

"But you think it's more than that? Is she

talking about killing herself? Or hurting herself?" Ms. Yu asks in her concerned counsellor voice.

"No! God! Danelle isn't suicidal for crying out loud! She's just unhappy." I gasp as I realize I've used Danelle's name. Damn, damn, damn! "She isn't talking about killing herself but I think she may be hurting herself," I say quickly, hoping Ms. Yu didn't notice.

I describe the finger picking and the strange marks I keep noticing on Danelle's arms. Ms. Yu studies me carefully as I talk, and occasionally makes a note on her pad.

"Is there anything else you can tell me?"

"Just that she's been leaving me these notes for the past two weeks," I tell her. I pull the tiny bits of paper out of my backpack and put them on the desk.

Ms. Yu smoothes them out and reads them. I study her office while she squints at the notes. She must be a favourite with the principal, because her office has a window and I know for a fact most offices at the school don't. She's got plants on the sill, and the shelves along the wall to my right are filled with more plants and tons of books.

Ms. Yu hands the notes back to me and I tuck them in my bag. Then I sit, waiting for her to tell me what to do next.

"I agree your friend sounds unhappy, Christine," she begins. "But if she won't come to me on her own and you don't think she's suicidal, I'm not sure what I can do." She taps a pencil against her desk, watching me. "Is there anything else unusual about her behaviour that you've noticed?"

"Well, she's been acting weird off and on for the last couple of months, actually," I confess. "She was really wingy just after Christmas, never sleeping, doing bizarre things like climbing the roof and disappearing to Seattle for a week. And she was doing dangerous stuff then too. And then she was fine, and now she's all depressed."

"Has she been...promiscuous?" Ms. Yu asks.

I'm surprised by this question but shake my head. "No, not really. She has an on-again off-again relationship with a real jerk, but I don't think she's sleeping with him."

"Okay. Well, did she talk to a doctor or a counsellor before, when she was acting manic?"

"No. She kept telling me I was trying to make her normal and she doesn't want to be normal. Could she be using? The symptoms I found on the Internet for drug use sound a lot like Danelle."

Ms. Yu smiles at me, the kind of smile an adult uses on an adorable toddler. "Christine, I understand you want to help your friend, but I'd be careful making diagnoses based on information you read on the Internet. You aren't a trained psychiatrist and these things are complicated. It could be depression or bipolar disorder or even just trouble at home."

"Mr. and Mrs. Mueller do work a lot and I know they've never understood Danelle..."

"See? There are lots of different things that can affect a person's behaviour. Please try to convince your friend to come and speak to me — that would be the best thing. Meanwhile, here's a pamphlet on teen depression and suicide. Come back if you have any more questions."

"Okay," I say, standing with my pamphlet. "Thanks anyway."

"You're a good friend, Christine, to be so concerned. And you've done the right thing in alerting someone who is trained to deal with this sort of thing."

Ms. Yu walks me to the main door of the counselling centre and says good-bye. I don't know what I had hoped for, but it was more than a pamphlet. Still, I guess it's kind of hard to help someone who doesn't want to be helped. I should know — I've been trying for months.

* * *

I've almost forgotten about my visit to the counsellor until a few days later when Ms. Yu approaches me in the hall.

"Hi, Christine," she says with a friendly smile. "I just wanted to check in with you and see how your friend is doing."

"About the same, I guess," I say. "I haven't seen much of her this week."

"Well, I found some more information on teen suicide and depression, and thought you might find it helpful." She hands me a small pile of booklets and pamphlets.

"Thanks." I glance around nervously at the other students filling the hall and Ms. Yu takes the hint.

"If you'd like to talk again, please come see me. Okay? I know it's hard to watch a loved one struggle and hurt, but you're a good friend. You did the right thing coming to me."

After she leaves, I shove the stack of papers into the bottom of my backpack.

Another note appears in my locker the next morning.

How could you? I thought you were my friend. I thought I could trust you. I saw you talking to that Ms. Yu person. I heard what she said! I was so embarrassed! I told you I'll be fine. It'll pass.

I sigh and slump against the lockers. Thanks a lot, Ms. Yu. Everything just keeps getting more and more complicated.

It's lunchtime before I find Danelle and corner her. "I'm sorry about what you overheard, Danelle," I say. "I was just... worried."

Danelle looks awful. Her clothes are soiled and creased. She hasn't washed her hair in a while and it hangs in oily strands off her shoulders. It looks like she tried to cut it herself with blunt scissors. Her eyes are huge and rimmed with dark shadows. But the worst of it is her hands. All eight fingers and both thumbs have been chewed and picked at.

The skin around her nails is raw and painful looking. How can she keep picking at them? Doesn't it hurt like hell?

"It's so embarrassing, Chris," she whispers, hugging herself.

"Danelle, I never meant to upset you. I just wanted to know how I could help you feel better. Honest. I'm so sorry you were embarrassed."

The bell rings and the halls slowly empty as students get to their afternoon classes. Soon Danelle and I are alone in the hallway. She is still holding herself and looking very forlorn. I reach out suddenly and put my arms around her, squeezing her tightly against me. She cries out in pain and pulls away from me.

"What?!" I cry, and she slowly peels back the sleeve of her shirt to reveal a nasty burn on her forearm. "What did you do?" I ask, recoiling from her.

"It was an accident," Danelle tells me, her eyes suddenly rimmed with tears. "I was using the curling iron and dropped it."

I look at the burn, trying not to gag, and then at my friend's face. Then I take her by the hand and drag her to the girls' washroom. She is almost cowering when I turn around.

"What the hell is with you?"

"Don't be mad at me," she begs, tears welling in her eyes. "I didn't want to bother you. I know you're busy with stuff. I can handle it all myself."

"No, Danelle, you can't. And you aren't bothering me. I'm your friend. I want to help. Just tell me what's going on. Are you taking something?"

"No, I'm not. Honest. I don't know what's wrong with me."

She sinks down the wall until she is sitting on the dirty linoleum, sobbing. I sit beside her, my hand on her back as she cries.

"I just feel like nothing matters, like I can't do anything," she tells me, her voice muffled by her arms. "I can't get up in the morning. I can't get enough sleep. I can't concentrate. Mr. Archer has warned me three times to get with it or I'm out of the show. I couldn't bear that!"

"Mr. Archer won't kick you out of the show. It's too close to performance time. But why didn't you just talk to me? Look at your hands, Danelle. Look at them!" I grab her hands and shake them in her face. I'm so angry, frustrated, and worried I don't know what to do. "This isn't normal!"

"I know. I'll try to stop," she says, pulling her hands away and tucking them carefully under her arms.

"And what about the burn? Have you got any more?" I ask, thinking suddenly of Ms. Yu's pamphlet and of the other scars I'd been noticing. My stomach lurches.

"No. It was an accident, honest," she says, beginning to cry again. "Honest."

"Danelle, you have to talk to someone. Maybe if you just talk to someone you'll figure out what the problem is and it can be fixed. I'm worried about you."

She looks at me through a haze of tears and wipes her nose on her sleeve. "I'm sorry. I'll try to get over it. I'll go and see that Ms. Yu person," she continues when she catches sight of my face. "Just don't be mad at me, okay? I can't stand for you to be mad at me."

I lean over and give her a careful hug, and gradually she stops crying. After a while we get up off the floor. Danelle washes her face and we go to class. A week later she is her old bubbly self and has forgotten all about her promise to see someone. She's even planning a party.

Chapter 12

"Are you interested in going to a party at Alana Wing's place on Saturday night?" I ask Jack. We are sitting in the library, books spread out around us. I have a bag of cookies tucked in my lap.

"I guess, sure. What's the occasion?" he asks, chewing as quietly as he can.

"Her brother Mike is having a birthday party, and Alana wants her friends there too." I don't tell him why Alana wants the moral support — that Cole will be there and she's hoping he might talk to her or even ask her to dance.

"Is Nutella going?" Jack asks. I scowl at him but he only grins. "Come on, Chris. The name is apt."

I can't argue with that. Since the beginning of the week Danelle has been called to the office twice, once for parading through the halls wearing only a bikini during an unseasonable cold spell (claiming that being cold was a case of mind over matter; if we thought we were hot, we would be) and once for chaining herself to the grill in the cafeteria to protest the serving of meat. Last weekend she had a miniature galaxy of stars tattooed on her right shoulder. And today she came to school with confetti stars sprinkled through her hair and is telling everyone to call her Ariel. She is wearing a brilliant red gypsy blouse and red and white striped pants.

She has been getting steadily more loony for the last two weeks: only eating green, white, or red foods; writing her own songs and singing them in the halls; joining Greenpeace and putting up posters in the halls at school; not sleeping; getting hauled home early in the morning by the cops for panhandling. Her parents are freaking out on her because the school keeps sending notes home. I knowing Danelle will graduate, but I don't know when she's getting any work done, as she's seldom at school for more than an hour at a time.

"Yes, Danelle is planning to go to Alana's. But with the way she's been acting, who knows if she'll show or if she'll stay."

Jack gives me a small, sympathetic smile and stuffs another cookie in his mouth. "I'll pick you up at eight," he says around chocolate chips.

* * *

The house is already pounding with music and talk when Jack and I arrive. We get sucked into the "vortex" (one of Danelle's words) and almost immediately are separated. I make my way to the kitchen, find something to drink, and go off in search of Alana. She's not upstairs so I head down to the basement.

I love this part of Alana's house. Her home is huge — I actually got lost trying to find my way to the bathroom the first time I was here. The basement has a guest bedroom with a private bath, an office for her father, who is a lawyer, and a large open area where they've got a bar, a pool table, a wide-screen TV with a full stereo system, and couches and chairs. Huge French doors lead outside to the patio. Talk about a perfect party house!

"You made it!" Alana cries when I finally find her sitting at the bar. She throws an arm around my neck. "I like the way you're wearing your hair. Did you do it yourself?"

I pat my up-do self-consciously. "It feels like it's going to topple over any second. Not to mention how exposed my neck feels. Watch out for guys with hatchets, will you?"

Alana laughs a bit too loudly and a bit too long, and I realize that she is either a little tipsy or very happy.

"He's here, isn't he?" I say, grinning. "And he talked to you? Invited you out?"

She turns several brilliant shades of pink and ducks her head. But she nods as well. I squeal like a little girl and grab her arm. "I can't believe you held out on me so long, Alana," I tell her.

"I was afraid to jinx it," she says, blushing for what is likely the hundredth time. "He hadn't ever said anything." She presses her hands together near her mouth, making her silver bracelets chime. She is absolutely quivering with excitement.

"I'm so jealous of you, you know," I confess. "Now I don't have a grad date."

"He hasn't asked me to grad!"

"He won't. You have to invite him. It's your grad." I down the last of my pop and set the empty can on the marble counter of the bar.

"I could never do that. Never."

"Guess you're stuck with me then. But that's okay, I'm sure he won't mind being left at home…"

Alana opens her mouth to respond but her words are drowned out as someone suddenly cranks the stereo. Music fills the crowded rec room like a pulsing wall of noise. Furniture is pushed back to the walls and people get up to dance. We look at each other and shrug.

The makeshift dance floor very quickly fills up. I see Danelle come down the stairs, drawn, I know, by the music. She catches sight of me and waves, but she is quickly on the dance floor with one of Mike's buddies, dancing as hard as she can.

It isn't long before Cole comes over. He is shy but very cute. Alana blushes yet again and has trouble making eye contact with him. I press myself back against the wall, trying to be inconspicuous, even though I don't think either of them notices me.

"Would you like to, you know, dance?" he says, finally, staring more at the floor than at Alana. With a tortured glance at me, Alana nods and slides off her stool.

"Why aren't you dancing, girl friend?" Danelle asks, swinging past me between songs.

She is flying high tonight. There are sparkles in her dark hair and she is wearing her gypsy costume. She can't stay still. Her hands flutter, her eyes twitch, and there's a low hum coming from her when she isn't speaking. She is so wired it's frightening.

"No one's asked me," I tell her, hoping she won't do anything insane tonight. My anxiety over her safety colours the whole evening.

"Do your own asking, Chris," she tells me, grabbing my hands and tugging. "Come on, who you going to ask? The cutey over there? Oooh, how 'bout Mike himself! He's a jock but he's smart. I like 'em smart. You got to give old Jack a run for his money or he's never going to make his move."

"No, thanks. I'm good watching. You dance."

I watch as my loony best friend finds herself a partner. Danelle presses herself up tightly against him and puts her arms around his neck. The counsellor's question about her being promiscuous rings in my ears as I watch her grind her hips against her partner's body. I feel my own face grow hot and turn my eyes away. Is this what Ms. Yu meant?

"You don't want to dance or anything, do you?" Jack asks, pulling my attention away from Danelle.

"How could I refuse an invitation like that?" I ask sarcastically. "You go ahead if you want, I'll just wait here."

"Come on, you're my date. You have to dance with me," he tells me, pulling me onto the dance floor.

Jack holds my hands and leads me around until I actually begin to relax and lose myself in the pulsing sounds. The music is fierce and fast, pounding through my brain, making my fingers tingle. Then the music changes to something slower, heavier. I close my eyes and Jack slips his arms around my waist. The music weighs me down and I cling a little tighter to Jack, leaning my head against his shoulder.

Jack is a good dancer, which is surprising, considering how awkward he can be just walking around. He hardly leads me at all, just guides me ever so slightly with his hands as we sway around the floor. I can feel his hands pressing against my back, feel his head touching mine. He is humming the tune softly, singing along when he knows the words. We've danced before, at school things, but never like this. He pulls back and I look up at him, smiling, happy. His face is very close. Too close. Way too close.

"I think I've had enough dancing for right now," I say, pulling away quickly.

I grab my purse and head in the general direction

of the stairs. I need light and talk and to get away from that hypnotizing music. I need to get away from Jack. My heart is pounding and my hands are damp with sweat. I stand in the kitchen and close my eyes for a second, trying to get myself under control.

What were you thinking? I ask myself, furious. We are friends. *FRIENDS*. And here I was, ready to kiss him. Kiss Jack. I can't calm the nervous flutter in my stomach and I think I might be sick. I wanted to kiss Jack. Kissing Jack would have ruined what we have, and I need him so badly as a friend right now.

"Are you okay?" he asks, appearing by my side. I make myself look at him, smile, nod.

"Just got a bit too warm down there. Sorry."

"You are sure you're okay? You look a little green."

"Yeah. I'll be fine."

"Maybe I should take you home," he says, still watching me, concerned.

I feel awful for worrying him. Did he feel it too? I don't think he did. Or he's a great actor.

"That would be good. Thanks. Sorry about this." I can't stop apologizing. I can't stop picturing Jack's mouth only centimetres from mine and thinking about how close I came to wrecking what we have.

Chapter 13

Monday afternoon, I arrive home from school just before three. Today was one of the longest days of my life. I felt like a twelve-year-old with her first crush — watching for Jack around every corner, blushing when he came over to say hi, hoping he'd accidentally brush my arm — it was awful. I want to crawl into bed and hide. I'm sure everyone noticed and is talking about it.

I'm not expecting anyone to be home — Katie has dance class and Mom works until five. But as I come through the front door I'm pretty sure I hear noises coming from upstairs. I freeze, my heart racing. A break-in?

I'm almost back out the door when I hear the murmuring again, followed by the very definite sound of Katie's giggle.

"What the hell is she doing home?" I mutter to myself, angry because I was so scared. I drop my bag in the kitchen and head upstairs to find out why Katie is not at dance class.

I pause just outside Katie's bedroom door. She's giggling again and I'm guessing she must be on the phone. I knock three times quickly and open the door.

"What the...?" I say and can't complete the sentence. I can't believe what I see.

Katie turns at my voice. Her eyes are huge, frightened behind the black mascara. She is sitting in the middle of the bed with the front of her shirt hanging open to the waist. Beside her, trying desperately to hide and failing, is some boy I have never seen before. He doesn't look much older than my sister, despite the million and a half rings and the tattoo on his right shoulder. I'm sure it is only a couple of seconds, but it feels like hours from the time I open her door to the time I close it again and go back downstairs.

Katie and her friend come slowly down the stairs, careful to look away from me sitting at the table. I look up ever so slightly and watch as Katie says good-bye and then stands there, one hand on the doorknob as though trying to decide whether or not to flee herself. Finally she lets go of the door and turns around. Her face is smudged, her lips puffy and red.

"So I guess you're going to blab your bloody mouth off, right? Anything to get me in trouble?" She stands in the doorway, her arms crossed.

I stare at her for a minute. "Are you sleeping with him?" I ask finally, ignoring her question. I can't help but think of Danelle dancing at the party, and of hearing later that she left with the guy she was dancing with.

Katie has the good sense to blush beet red at my question. "That's none of your bloody business!" she screams. "I'm old enough to make my own choices!"

"YOU'RE FOURTEEN YEARS OLD, for God's sake! You're a baby! You want to end up with a kid? Huh? Is that what you want? You don't know what the hell you're doing, Katie, and neither does Lover Boy."

"YOU'RE JUST JEALOUS!" she screams, her hands clenched in fists, her face still red. "I'm not you, Prissy Chrissy! Just because you can't get a date! God, you are such a prig. You can't stand it that I might be getting some and you aren't! You can't even get dumb old Jack interested in you, you're so pathetic!"

The sting of those words is so sharp I almost double over. I stare at her blankly for half a second, then I turn and head for the stairs. Behind me, I can hear my sister breathing and the footsteps on the floor as she follows me.

"Christine," she says but I don't stop. "Christine, I'm sorry. I shouldn't have said that. Look, we weren't doing anything but necking, honest. I wouldn't go all the way. You know that. I'm not a fool."

I turn around and we look at each other. We both know a line has been crossed somewhere, and I think we both know it shouldn't have been. I don't know my little sister anymore and that worries me, because it looks to me like she's becoming an awful lot like Danelle.

* * *

There is a letter from the Richmond Arts Council, waiting for me on Thursday. Several weeks ago, Ms. Armstrong convinced me to apply for a scholarship they have every year. I thought she was nuts, but I sent in the portfolio of writing to keep her from nagging me.

I stand in the empty kitchen, holding the envelope, unwilling to open it. I don't want to read "Thank you for your interest." I don't want to be shot down. It was stupid to send it in the first place. Ms. Armstrong was wrong. I'm just kidding myself about my ability and, come September at UBC, I'll know for sure I am.

"What's so interesting?" Katie comes up behind me so quietly I jump and drop the letter. Before I can react, she has scooped it up and is staring at it. "What's this?"

"A letter, for me," I say and reach for it.

Katie and I have had an uneasy truce since our fight on Monday, and the fragility of it is making us both very careful with each other.

"Aren't you going to open it?" she asks, handing it back to me.

"It's from the Arts Council," I explain, running

my tongue over my very dry lips. "I applied for a writing scholarship. They're just writing to tell me thanks for trying."

My sister frowns hard at me. "Why do you do that?"

"Do what?"

"Put yourself down all the time. It's bloody annoying. Guys would like you a whole lot more if you were more positive about yourself."

She takes an apple from the fridge and stands there, obviously waiting for me to do something. Finally I get up the nerve to open the letter:

"*Dear Christine; The Scholarship Committee of the Community Arts Council of Richmond takes great pleasure in informing you that you have been chosen as one of this year's recipients of their annual scholarships...*" There is more but I can't read it — the words are a blur.

I am crying. They chose me! I stare and stare at the words on the page, although I can't read them through my tears. "I got it," I whisper to Katie. "I GOT IT!"

She grabs me and we dance around the kitchen, waving the precious letter in the air.

* * *

I can't reach Danelle. I try most of Thursday evening, I watch for her at school on Friday, but she's nowhere to be found. By Friday night, I don't even want to tell her my news anymore.

What kind of a friend is she anyway? I'm always there for her, always! And the one time in my life when something special and important happens, she does a disappearing act.

"Where the hell have you been?" I yell at her when she finally returns my calls late Friday night. "I've been trying to find you for two days. I wanted to tell you I won the scholarship." Even though I'm angry, I feel a happy glow from saying it out loud one more time.

"The scholarship?" she repeats vaguely.

"For creative writing. You know, I write stories." I want to shake her. What the hell is going on with her? Can't she ever be there for me?

"That's really great, Chris," she says, but doesn't sound the least bit convincing.

"What is wrong with you, Danelle? Huh? Can't you just be happy for me? Can't things ever be about me?"

"There was this party," she says, interrupting me. "And I…did…some stuff…"

I stop my tirade and close my eyes for a second before I ask, "Where are you, Danelle?"

"I'm at Brian's now. His roommates are all away and he's just gone to get some beer or something. But I can't stay here, Chris," she whispers, crying now. Her sobs soften my heart and my anger starts changing into fear for her. "I've got to leave before he gets back."

"How? Do you have a car?" My mother comes to the door of my room, her eyes questioning.

"No. I'll walk."

"Screw that. It's late and Brian doesn't live in the best area. Wait there. I'll come get you, okay? Just wait there."

I quickly hang up and pull on some clothes. Mom hands me the car keys and goes to explain to my father why I'm taking off with the car at eleven o'clock at night.

* * *

Somehow I convince my parents to let Danelle stay the weekend. She sleeps pretty much the whole time and doesn't get up for school Monday morning. She's up when I get home that afternoon, though, and we sit at the kitchen table while I eat something. She looks less freaked than she did Friday night, and she's very calm.

"Did you call your parents?" I ask.

"Yeah. I told them it was a last-minute thing. They did their usual twenty questions, but…" She shrugs. "And I called Brian. I told him I went home because I wasn't feeling well."

"What did he say?"

"Not much." She picks up a napkin from the table and plays with the fringed edge. She doesn't say anything for a long time, then looks up at me suddenly. "He wanted to know if we were still on for next weekend."

"Are you?"

"I guess," she says and shrugs. "Anyway, I better

get going home. Tell your mom and dad thanks for the bed — I appreciate it. And thanks, you know, for helping me out, Chris. I'll see you tomorrow, okay?"

I see her to the door and watch as she walks down the driveway. When she gets to the corner she waves a little wave and then she's gone. And it isn't until she's out of my sight that I realize I never once asked her what kind of "stuff" she did. And I also realize that I really don't want to know.

Chapter 14

I don't see Danelle the next day, as it turns out. I wait for a couple of minutes at our usual meeting place, but I've gotten so used to her not showing that I don't wait long. I figure she'll eventually find me at school, full of excuses. But she doesn't show up at all that day. I call her mid-morning but no one answers.

I head home at the end of the day by myself. I've got piles of work waiting, and it's my night to make dinner, but for half an hour I just sit at the kitchen table, eating crackers and cheese and reading a novel I started ages ago and still haven't finished.

Around four o'clock the phone rings, startling me from the world of my book and making me whack my knee on the table. I hobble to the phone, rubbing my throbbing knee.

"Hello?" Silence on the other end. Not even breathing. "Hello, who is this?" I ask, getting ready to hang up. Then I hear what sounds like a small cough. "Is someone there?"

"Christine?"

The voice is so low, so tiny and weak, I almost don't hear it. A little prickle of fear crawls up my back. "Danelle? What's going on?"

"Chris, I wanted to say good-bye," she says.

My fear is working its way into a full panic attack. Something is really wrong. "Danelle! What's wrong, where are you?"

"I just wanted to say good-bye," Danelle says in that voice that is, but isn't, hers.

"You have to tell me where you are," I try again. "Are you at home?"

"Yes, but don't come. It's better this way."

The phone goes dead, and for a long, long, terrifying second I sit staring at the receiver in my hand. Danelle has done something to herself, I know it, and I can't even move. I sit holding the phone and breathing long, choking breaths for nearly a minute before I manage to replace the phone and get off the chair.

No one answers my frantic banging on the Muellers' front door, but it's unlocked. I run inside, calling loudly to Danelle. I can hear the fear in my voice and I'm afraid I'll be sick. I thunder up the stairs and throw open the door to Danelle's bedroom. The curtains are tightly drawn and the blinds are pulled down. A little light comes in from the hall, but in the bedroom there is only the eerie glow of the fluorescent galaxy across the ceiling. Danelle's breathing is very shallow and her skin is damp, clammy, cold. She doesn't open her eyes when I touch her.

"Okay, okay," I talk to myself, trying to breathe normally, trying to think straight. Danelle needs a doctor, a hospital. The phone is lying on the floor beside Danelle's bed. Forcing myself to breathe deeply and stay calm, I dial 911 and ask for an ambulance.

"Okay, I'm sending you one. Can you tell me what the problem is?" the voice on the other end asks. I breathe and swallow.

"My friend, my friend has tried to kill herself."

The words stick in my throat and I cough, fighting back tears. The voice asks another question and I wipe my eyes, sniffing as I look around, finally finding a small, empty vial on the bed.

"Pills, some kind of pills,"

"Can you read the label?"

My fingers shake as I try to find the name on the bottle. My eyes are getting used to the lack of light, but I can't read the label without switching on the lamp. The phone falls from my shoulder and I pick it up, apologizing into it.

"That's okay, just take it easy. The ambulance is coming."

"She took 'acetaminophen with codeine,'" I say, reading the label. "Please hurry! She's breathing real funny and her skin is all cold and clammy."

"Do you know how long ago she took them, Christine?"

At some point the voice must have asked for my name but I don't remember that question. I try to think about what time it was when Danelle phoned me. "Four o'clock. She called me then and she sounded kind of awful. She was like this, unconscious, when I got here."

"Do you have any idea how many pills she might have taken, Christine?" the voice asks. I shake my head and whisper a soft "no" into the phone.

I touch Danelle's face and smooth back the damp hair, then the tears I've been forcing back will not be held any longer. The phone falls away from my ear as I lean against the bed on the floor and cry. Behind me, Danelle's breathing slows some more. She is dying. My best friend is lying there dying and maybe I am too late, maybe I haven't saved her.

The ambulance attendants arrive, beautiful to me in their black pants and white coats. They move me gently aside and bend over Danelle's body. Carefully, carefully, they lift her onto the stretcher and move out of the room and down the stairs. Someone asks if I want to ride in the ambulance and I climb in the front seat. Somehow my seatbelt is fastened and the door is shut and the siren is going and we are driving through traffic to the hospital, with Danelle dying in the back.

* * *

I am at the hospital for a long time but the doctors won't let me see her. She won't see her own parents, who sit in horrified silence in the waiting room, holding each other tightly. In the end, Mom takes me home. It's the last place I want to be, but where else is there?

I pick at the food Katie puts in front of me, avoiding her sympathetic eyes, and escape to my bedroom. It's nearly nine o'clock when Katie brings me the phone. "It's Jack," she whispers.

"Thank God you called," I say, knowing I'm going to cry very soon. "Danelle's in the hospital. She took some pills, tried…" I choke on the words, "to kill herself this afternoon, But she's going to live."

"Holy, Christine. Are you all right?" he asks, and I feel the first tears break free and slide down my cheeks.

"I'll be okay."

"Do you know what happened?"

"No. I didn't see her again before I left the hospital. I don't know why she did it."

"It'll be okay. It will. They'll make her get help now."

"Yeah, they will, won't they?" I sniff and wipe at my running nose. "Are you still at work?"

"I'm done and I'm on my way over. Just hold tight," he says, and is gone.

* * *

I am at the hospital the next morning as soon as they allow visitors. I carry a huge balloon and a basket of flowers, as cheerful as I could find. I stand outside Danelle's door for a long time, composing myself, trying to ignore the hospital smell and sounds. I bury my nose in the carnations and push open the door.

Danelle is in the bed closest to the window. She is staring out at the parking lot and doesn't hear me until I'm almost beside her bed. I expected tubes, wires, monitors — but there is only one intravenous tube running from the drip bag beside the bed into the back of her left hand. She is whiter than the sheets, and her eyes are ghostly gray and huge in her face. She looks beaten.

"You're here." She smiles at me, a fragile smile that doesn't quite fully form.

I set the balloon on the table and place the flowers beside it. She reaches out and touches the balloon, making it bob slightly.

"They're beautiful. Thank you." Her voice is raspy and hard to hear.

I know they pumped her stomach and Mom warned me how rough she would look. But still, it is not what I imagined.

"How are you feeling?"

Danelle shrugs and coughs slightly. "You found me," she says, catching my eyes and holding them with her own dark ones. She says it like an accusation. "You should have left me."

"Don't you dare say that to me!" I cry, my hand

114

flying to cover my mouth. "How could you think I'd leave you? After you phoned me… to say, to say good-bye? How could you think I wouldn't come?"

"Christine, don't. Don't cry, please," Danelle begs me, grabbing my hand and holding it. I sink into the chair at the side of the bed and bury my face in the blankets. "It's all just so hard. So hard. And it never goes away," she rasps, keeping hold of my hand.

"Then let the doctors help you." I sit up, wiping at my damp face. "Let the psychiatrists help you get better."

"Yeah, they've been in. But what can I tell them? Huh? That I did it 'cause my boyfriend dumped me?" She shakes her head. "It just got to be too much. All of it." She closes her eyes and rolls her head away from me.

"You've got to let them try, Danelle," I tell her softly, pleading. "You've got to let them try."

Chapter 15

After a couple of days Danelle is released from the hospital and sent home with medication and a referral to a therapist. I am caught in a mix of emotions — mostly relief that she will finally get help and that perhaps her strange behaviour of the past year will be figured out, but also fear. If she tried to kill herself once, what's to say it won't happen again? And what if she doesn't call the next time?

She seems okay: making plans, actually attending school, neither way too high nor way too low, seeing her therapist. But she won't talk about any of it — not the suicide attempt, not the depression or Brian, and not the wild stuff either — with me. If I bring it up she shuts me down with a warning look.

Perhaps it's selfish of me, but I need to talk about what happened, to work through it. I feel like I'm walking on broken glass with her, that one misplaced step will result in further injury, and I hate it. I want some reassurance that she's working at getting better, but she flatly refuses to talk about it.

We bring our yearbooks home and sit in my room to look at them. Danelle is engrossed in reading the comments beneath each grad's picture but I can't concentrate on it. I'm not happy with the way things are between us. I'm tired of Danelle dictating how we'll be friends. I am trying to figure out how to bring up the taboo subject when Danelle lets out a huge laugh.

"What?"

"This comment — what a goof Arvid is," she says, shaking her head. "And he thinks he's going to be a doctor."

"Speaking of doctors," I begin slowly, knowing I'm on dangerous ground, but seeing an opening. "How are things with your therapist?"

Danelle doesn't answer me right away. She studies the yearbook, her dark hair blocking her face from my view. "Why do you need to know?" Her voice is sharp edged.

"I don't need to know, I guess. I was just wondering how things are going, if the medication is working, if you're feeling better."

"Better?" she parrots. "I've got doctors poking around in my brain, my parents always in my face, watching my every move. I'm so spaced-out on those stupid pills they're making me take that half the time I can't even think straight. How is any of that better?"

"Things'll improve, Danelle," I try, speaking softly. "I know it must be hard right now…"

"Stop it, Christine!" she yells at me, throwing her yearbook across the room. It hits the closet door with a thud and falls to the floor. "Just stop trying to look after everything all the time. I can't stand it anymore. This is all your fault in the first place. If you'd just left me alone, just let me *die* when I wanted to, everything would be fine. But this, this is just shit."

I step back, struck by her words. "You don't mean that, Danelle. You can't mean that! And how could you think for one minute I'd leave you to die when you called to say good-bye? You wanted me to find you. You wanted to get help!"

"No, you just wanted to 'fix' me again, like you've been trying to do all year. Well, you got your wish; I have to see a bloody doctor now. Maybe her magic pills will make me more 'normal.' You must be thrilled."

We are standing, facing each other across the room, and the air is heavy with the heat of the afternoon and our words. We are both breathing heavily. Danelle slips her hand into her pocket and pulls out a small prescription vial. She glances at it for a minute, shakes it.

"You know what? I'm not doing this anymore. I'm tired of everyone overreacting to every little thing I do. You can take your pills and your doctor and go to hell." She drops the bottle on the floor and slams out of the room. I stare at the closed door for a long time, then I slowly slide down the wall until I can't slide any further, bury my head in my arms, and cry.

I cry for a long time, long past the time I'm exhausted and my sobs are dry and painful. Then very slowly, but deliberately, I climb on the bed. The first star comes off easily. Just a little wiggle of my fingernail under the edge and it flutters slowly to the bed, landing on the pillow. I watch it fall, then look back up at the ceiling. There, where the little star was, is an ugly white hole where the paint has peeled away with the back of the sticker. Danelle's words of so many months ago come back to me: "It isn't as though they're permanent."

The next star is harder to get off. It rips several times. My anger rises with each failed attempt to remove it, until I am tearing at it, my fingers getting sore and raw. The star finally comes free and I move to the next one, my anger driving me along, faster and faster and faster. Around my feet is a puddle of yellow. No celestial body now, no parallel galaxy, just a mess at my feet, a mess in my mind and heart.

I am crying again by the time I get to the last star. My neck hurts — from holding it at such an awkward angle — and my back too. My throat hurts from crying, my fingers from tugging and ripping. Everything hurts, everything.

Chapter 16

Danelle calls the next afternoon in the middle of my television marathon. "I just wanted to, you know, ask forgiveness for what I said. It's not your fault — I was just having an off day."

"Okay."

"Christine, are we okay? I said I was sorry."

"You did. I appreciate that." I hang up and go back to my reruns.

I am so very tired: tired of carrying the weight of Danelle's illness on my shoulders, tired of loving Jack with no hope he'll love me back as more than a friend, tired of my life. I find it amazingly easy to lie on the couch in front of the television and stare blankly at the images on the screen for hours on end. I get up and go to school when I have to, but that's about it. I avoid Alana, Danelle, and especially Jack. I make up lies and they leave me alone.

I fight with myself, though. Shouldn't I try to

force Danelle to take her pills? Force her to keep seeing the therapist? I just want her to be well, to be her old self again. But I don't know how to make her see that, and I'm too tired to keep up the struggle.

My parents are called out of town to a funeral in Calgary. They leave Katie and me with a long list of expectations and warnings. I can see they are reluctant to go. My mother is doing her squinting thing at me. I smile as convincingly as I can and eventually they leave us. I wave them off and return to my spot on the couch.

One afternoon Katie wanders downstairs and stands at the end of the couch, staring at the crap I have on the TV. "What's this?" she asks finally, sitting at the other end of the sofa with her legs curled beneath her.

"Dunno."

"Mind if I watch with you?"

"Suit yourself."

"You know I've been growing my hair out," she says a while later.

I lift my head ever so slightly to look at her. I notice, for the first time, that the clips are gone. And that she has changed her hair back to its natural colour. We are both blondes, with hair that is wavy and thick. Katie's is just long enough now to reach below her ears, giving her a pixie-like look.

"I thought, you know, since I'm going into grade ten in the fall, I should try something new. Plus, Steve said he liked your hair," she adds when I don't answer.

"Who's Steve?" I ask, interested despite myself.

"Oh, some guy I met at the pool a couple of weeks ago. He's in grade ten at Richmond High. He plays basketball for them."

"Must be tall then," I say, turning back to the TV. "You'll need a stool to reach his lips."

Katie laughs then, a loud, clear, ringing sound, and I find myself giggling with her. But laughing takes more energy than I have. It's easier to just sit. After a while Katie gets up and leaves. I sink back into the cushions and stare at the television.

I am unprepared when she comes back later and tells me I have a visitor.

"Tell whoever it is I'm not decent."

"Too late," Jack says. He is standing in the doorway looking tanned and healthy and beautiful. I look back at the television.

"What's going on, Chris?" he asks, sitting down beside me on the couch. "You keep avoiding me at school, you won't answer the phone."

"I'm really tired, Jack. I don't feel like visitors."

"It's Danelle, isn't it? Katie told me the two of you had a huge blow up last week."

"My sister needs to keep her mouth shut."

"Your sister cares about you. She was worried."

He puts his arm around my shoulder and pulls me over against him. I don't want him touching me but am powerless to push him away. I cry instead, soaking the front of his black T-shirt with my tears. I hate that he is seeing me like this but I can't stop. And when I am done crying I tell him everything.

"Holy, Christine. That girl is a piece of work."

"She called to apologize the next day," I tell him, wiping at my damp face. "But nothing's changed, Jack. That's the thing. She won't take her medication and she doesn't think she needs a doctor. So what's going to change?"

We sit together for a long time, my head on his shoulder, his arm around me, and after a while I fall asleep.

I spend a lot of time over the next couple of weeks with Alana and Jack. We hang out at the pool, go to movies or downtown. Neither one makes demands on me and gradually my exhaustion fades. It is such a relief to be friends with Alana. She is sane, calm, happy, and giving. We talk about everyday things — school in the fall, summer jobs, graduation, her new boyfriend, the change in Katie — and the conversation is normal and logical.

"So Katie actually went and got a job?" Alana asks one day in early June.

"Isn't it amazing? She's babysitting, too, of all things. Every day after school for two hours. I didn't even know she liked little kids. It's great having the house to myself."

"She's really changed, huh?"

I nod thoughtfully. From freakish twit my sister has morphed into this beautiful, intelligent person. She's going to school and to dance class, babysitting, helping out at home. I must admit that her behaviour was freaking me out; she was acting way too much like Danelle. But it must have just been a phase. Maybe Danelle's suicide attempt scared her. Who knows? I'm just glad to have my sister back. We even went to the movies together last weekend.

"I'm glad you're feeling better too. I didn't like seeing you so depressed," Alana says softly a few minutes later. She is studying me over the top of her geography book.

"Well, I wasn't really depressed," I tell her slowly. "Not like Danelle. I can't even imagine what it must have been like for Danelle, feeling so horrible she wanted to die."

I've thought about that a lot in the last few weeks. I can't ever know what life is like for Danelle when she's in one of her depressions — or on her highs, either — but my own life doesn't seem nearly so overwhelming in comparison.

Since our blow up we've been keeping our distance, and that's the way I want it right now. She appears to be okay, going to class, acting normal, but I don't know if she's taking her pills or if she's seeing the doctor. I can't take care of her anymore. She's going to have to do it herself — or not, if that's her choice. The realization frees me.

* * *

The time I spend with Jack is wonderful and awful at the same time. He asks nothing of me, but I want so much more from him than just his friendship that it's painful. Sometimes, when we're alone and quiet together, he'll look at me and I wonder if he ever sees a girl, instead of just Christine. I am trying to resign myself to always being his friend and never his girlfriend, but it isn't easy.

"Danelle told me she's taking her medication again," I tell him. It's a hot June afternoon and we are hanging off the edge of the pool at his town-house complex.

"Well, that's a good thing."

I shrug. Who knows how long it'll last. "She's been bugging me to see her. She says I'm spending all my time with you and Alana these days."

"Is that a problem?" he asks, resting his head on his arms. "Because I'm…"

"No," I say quickly, alarmed. "I… I need to spend time with you and Alana. I can't cope with Danelle right now."

"I'm right here," Jack says. "Besides, it's been good, just hanging out together."

"Yeah, it's been nice." I grin at him, and then close my eyes while I float, feeling happier and freer than I have in months.

When I open my eyes Jack's face is right there, close like it was when we were dancing. The urge to kiss him is so strong, I feel myself lean toward him even as my brain is telling me to stop. Our lips almost touch before I pull back, awkward and apologizing.

"I'm sorry, that was stupid," I begin, unable to face him. My face is flaming and I long to sink beneath the surface of the pool.

"No, I'm sorry, I shouldn't have done that," he says. "It's just that I've wanted to for so long."

"You have?" I ask in stunned disbelief.

"Yeah," he says, speaking against the tiled edge of the pool. "Ever since we went to my dad's after Angela was born. I know we're just friends! It won't happen—"

"Jack," I say, interrupting him with a hand on his shoulder. "It's okay, I wanted you to." My heart is racing and my mouth is dry. I can't believe we're having this conversation.

"You did? How long?"

"Mike's party. When we were dancing."

We stare at each other for a long time, stupid grins plastered on our faces. All this time and he was feeling the same way I was.

"What were you going to do?" he asks softly, touching my face. I am liquid inside as he leans forward, his lips seeking my lips. We kiss softly and he pulls away, smiling at me, then leans in again and crushes his mouth against mine. He wraps his arms around my waist and holds me as though he's never going to let me go.

Chapter 17

"I never thought we'd actually get here," I say to Alana and Jack. We are lounging in my backyard, trying to get some sun before the dance tonight.

Alana grins up at me, nodding. "Tell me about it. Graduation. A boyfriend, for each of us," she says, winking at Jack. "Scholarships. This is what we've been waiting for."

"It is going to be one righteous weekend, I promise," Jack tells me. I know it will be.

I am so excited I can hardly stand it. The grad dance is in six hours. There are parties planned all weekend. I've been waiting for this for so long, and now that it's here, it's going to be better than I hoped. Jack and I are going together, as a couple, with Alana and Cole. Danelle is going with some guy she met a month ago. She's been taking her medication for a few weeks and has promised me she'll keep taking it. We are spending a bit more time together, and so far things have been okay.

"How do you think you're going to get your hair arranged?" Alana asks, but before I can answer her the phone rings.

"I had to tell you! I met the most awesome guy last night, Christine," Danelle says, her words tumbling over themselves. I feel little tremors of recognition run up and down my back. "He's in second year science at UBC, going to be an engineer. He was in on the last engineer's prank. Remember? When they hung a car from the bridge? Anyway, his name's Sebastian and he's the greatest kisser! Oh, my God! I can't believe I ever thought Brian was a good kisser. We talked for ages and danced, and made out, you know. You'll never guess where we are! Sebastian is taking me bungee jumping! Isn't that awesome! I'm so excited. I've always wanted to try this. He's just gone to get tickets but I had to call and tell you. I think I'm going to try a swan dive from the platform, what do you think? Or maybe they'll let me go backwards. Do you think they'll let me go backwards?"

"What about grad, Danelle?" I can't do this anymore.

"Oh! We'll make it. It's not till later anyway. And first I have got to try this! I am so psyched!"

Her words trail off as I stop listening. I meet Jack's eyes and feel my own fill with sudden tears. *She promised*, I keep thinking. She promised to give the medication a chance and she lied to me.

"I have to go, Danelle." I hang up quickly and clear my throat as I return to my friends. Alana gives me a sympathetic glance and Jack comes over to hug me.

"Danelle," he states against my hair.

"Yes. She and Sebastian — her new friend — are going bungee jumping."

"Is she…?"

"Yes."

* * *

By five o'clock that afternoon, I have pushed Danelle and her adventures from my mind. I've had my hair and nails done. I'm in my beautiful blue dress. I am ready to have a good time. Jack arrives with Cole and Alana in the limousine and we stand in the front yard having pictures taken. We are just about to climb in the car when Katie comes running out of the house.

"It's Danelle. She says she *has* to talk to you." I take the phone reluctantly.

"Would you believe those assholes wouldn't let me jump?" she says, yelling into the phone so I have to hold it away from my ear. "They have some stupid-ass rule about being eighteen to jump without a parent's permission. Can you believe that! I am so pissed off!"

"Danelle, where are you? Where's Sebastian?"

"Oh, Sebastian. What a jerk he turned out to be. He said I was embarrassing him by yelling at the bungee guy, that he couldn't help the rules, that he'd get in trouble if he broke them, lose his job. Like I care! It's a stupid rule! I told Sebastian to find another place but he said no. He was taking me home! God, what a jerk! But I can do it myself. I figured out how, bought all the stuff I need — I checked on the Internet — and I even have a helmet!"

Fear rips through me. "Danelle, what are you talking about?"

"It's a surprise! Bring your camera and come watch! Maybe I'll get in the paper! Or on the TV! Wouldn't that be cool?"

Her voice is high-pitched, her words tripping out of her mouth. She keeps talking while I desperately try to think of something to say to stop her from doing whatever it is she has planned. She'll kill herself. This time she will kill herself.

"Where are you going?"

"Will you come then? And watch? I want you to watch, Chris. You could even call the paper! Meet me at the Lions Gate Bridge," she says in a rush of words. And then the phone is dead.

I hang up and turn to look at the people gathered on the lawn in front of me: Jack and Cole in their handsome black tuxedos, Alana in her floor-length silver dress. How can Danelle ruin this weekend for me?

"I think Danelle is going to try and bungee jump from the Lions Gate Bridge," I tell them, hearing how ridiculous it sounds. "I have to stop her."

We let Alana and Cole take the limousine, and my parents lend Jack and me their car. I sit with my hands clenched between my knees as Jack drives downtown to Stanley Park. He glances at me every once in a while, and twice he touches my cheek gently, but he doesn't say anything and I'm very grateful. If he speaks I will cry, and if I cry I may not stop.

We make it to the causeway leading into Stanley Park, but it's rush hour and the cars are inching toward the bridge. I'm praying that Danelle will wait for me to get there.

The lush beauty of Stanley Park usually impresses me, but today all I can think of is that there are too many trees, too much road, too many people. I'm pushing with my high-heel-encased right foot as if I can push the car toward the bridge.

Finally we round the last curve and there, in front of us, are the stone lions standing guard over Burrard Inlet and the bridge. There is nowhere to park legally, but Jack pulls over as soon as he can, even though the car is straddling the curb. He leaves the emergency flashers on as we climb out.

With me in my ankle-length blue gown and silver heels, and Jack in his black tuxedo and cummerbund, we are not dressed for this. I can feel the heads turning to look out of car windows as we make our way onto the bridge sidewalk.

I'm so tired of this. Tired of the lies and the broken promises and the denial. Tired of running to the rescue, or picking up the pieces when I don't get there in time. I love Danelle but I can't do this anymore.

"There she is," Jack says, pointing up ahead of us. I follow his finger and see her, about fifty metres away.

"Oh, my God, Jack. She's going to kill herself," I say, envisioning her floating face-down in the murky waters below us, or smashed on the rocks.

Danelle has an old bike helmet on her head, the straps hanging unfastened down the sides of her face. Harnesses criss-cross her chest and waist, and she has attached metal fasteners on both shoulder straps. She grins as we approach, and claps her hands like a small child.

"I knew you'd come! Isn't this amazing? This'll be perfect, really. The wind is good, it's plenty light out. I just have to make sure there aren't any boats underneath! Where's the reporter? And the TV guys? Are they coming? Did you call them? Jack, you look like a penguin in that tux! What's with the clothes? You guys eloping?"

"Danelle, it's grad tonight. Remember? You were going with Dave?"

She blinks at me for a second then shakes her head. "Right! That. Of course, if you like that kind of thing. This'll be so much more provocative! You are going to try with me, right? I mean, I'll go first then when you pull me back up, you guys can take a turn. It'll be even funnier with those costumes you're wearing! Your dress will go right over your head, Chris — hope you're wearing underwear!"

"Danelle, please, stop for a second and think

about this," I begin, reaching out a hand to her. She pulls back from me and her eyes flash with sudden anger.

"Don't you even think about it, Christine Dawson!" she cries, clutching her rope tightly to her chest. "You aren't spoiling this for me!

As she speaks, Danelle backs away, staying out of grabbing range. Her eyes dart left and right. She's fluttering and humming like a hummingbird. I have never seen her this agitated before and I'm suddenly more frightened than I was even when she disappeared. I grip Jack's hand as tightly as I can and in response I hear the numbers on the phone beep as he dials 911.

"Danelle, I'm not trying to stop you, honest," I lie. "I just want to make sure you've thought it all out and are going to be safe." My heart is pounding and my hands are damp with sweat, but slowly I walk toward her again, leaving Jack behind me.

"I thought it all out! I can do this. It's going to be great! See, I've got all the rope here," she says, holding the thick beige rope out for us to see. "And these pieces attach to my harnesses. I'm going to tie the rope to the beam here, see? It's good springy rope so I get good bounce. I had a good look at the bungee-jumping place. I know exactly how they do it all."

She is managing to stay away from me, and every once in a while she coils more rope into her arms. She has a lot of rope.

"Do you know how far the drop is?"

"Oh, sure. The cruise ships go under here and they're about a hundred metres high, right? So I just subtracted a bit. Don't want to get wet, right?"

My God, I think. She has no clue how far down the water is. A horn honks and Danelle jumps about a foot in the air, her eyes wide, her pupils fully dilated. She is far beyond sane right now. My brain starts jumping in a thousand directions, trying to think of a way of keeping her on the sidewalk until the police come.

The cars are beginning to slow as they pass us — and why wouldn't they? Two girls on the side of the bridge — one dressed for a fancy party, the other in harnesses and a bike helmet — and the guy behind us in a tuxedo. If anything's worthy of television cameras, it's this scene.

Danelle kneels down and paws through her coils of rope, muttering under her breath. She finds the end and holds it up triumphantly. "Let's get this show on the road!"

"Why'd you stop taking your pills, Danelle?"

She looks up at me as though she forgot I was there, rocking toe-to-heel and bouncing slightly. Her hands flutter. "The pills," she says. "Those pills made me feel lousy. And that doctor! God, I hate doctors — they're always trying to stuff you in some little round hole! I'm a free spirit! I'm not 'bipolar' or manic or whatever the hell words they use!" While we're talking she has fastened the end of the rope to a beam of the bridge. My heart races.

I think I hear sirens in the distance, but when I

listen again there is only the noise of traffic and the occasional honking horn or loudmouth calling out his car window. But then I see the lights, coming from the north behind Danelle, and relief washes through me in waves. But I can't focus on the police because Danelle has finished tying her rope.

"I'm ready!" she announces suddenly and starts to climb the railing, coils of rope looping around her. "You come right over here close so you can pull me up when I stop bouncing."

"I'm not strong enough to pull you up, Danelle!"

"Well, where's Lover Boy?" she asks, scanning the sidewalk for Jack. "What the hell?" she says, and I turn to see two police officers approaching slowly from the south. Jack catches my eye and just the sight of him, waiting for me, helps. I turn back to Danelle.

"Who called the cops?!" she screams, climbing further up the railing. "Well, I'm going! You boys can just stay where you are! I've been planning this! I thought it all out! You—"

"I called the police, Danelle," I yell above the noise of her ranting. "*I* called."

She stops climbing and stares down at me, her face flushed. "You called? I thought you were my friend! Friends don't rat each other out!"

The two officers who have been approaching us from the north have almost reached Danelle now. I glance at them and realize one of them isn't a cop, but a civilian. Then I see the needle: he's a nurse. Tears fill my eyes but I choke them down. I really can't do this anymore. It has to stop. Someone has to stop her.

"You'll kill yourself if you jump off the side of this bridge and I care about you too much to let that happen."

My eyes track everything as the cop behind Danelle lunges at her at the same time that she turns out over the water and lets herself fall. Screams fill the air, and I'm pushed left and right as cops rush past me trying to get to Danelle. I stand, staring at the empty space on the railing where Danelle just stood, and clamp a hand over my mouth to stop myself from screaming. Then strong arms have me tight and I bury my face in Jack's chest and cry.

"Let me go, you bastards!"

"Careful of her head!"

"I know what I'm doing! Get the hell off me! I'm not crazy!"

"Got her? Here, hang on while I untangle this mess."

"What was she thinking?"

They finally manage to pull her onto the bridge, although it takes all three officers to hold her still once they get her to safety.

"There, there, my friend, take it easy. We're going to get you someplace safe. No one's going to hurt you. You just relax," the nurse, a huge poster boy for bodybuilding, says soothingly. But

Danelle won't be soothed. She glares at me with so much hatred I take a step back.

"YOU BITCH! I HATE YOU!! I HATE YOUR GUTS! I'M NOT CRAZY!" she screams, and then there is silence as she slumps into the arms of the cop.

"Oh God, Jack, what have I done?" I whisper, stunned by the sight of my best friend being lifted into the arms of a psychiatric nurse. The entire scene is surreal. Danelle is still wearing her bike helmet and the harnesses, and her head lolls back against the nurse's arm. The rush and roar of traffic is all around us, and from beneath the bridge comes the mournful cry of a tugboat.

"You did what you had to do, Chris," he tells me, rubbing my back as they carry my best friend to the waiting ambulance.

Epilogue

I stare at the same blank page for half an hour. Every time I type words, I end up deleting them. I have assignments due for three different classes, but I am sitting here unable to get anything out. I'm not sure what's wrong with me. I can hear my sister and my dad laughing and talking to each other outside as they rake the leaves from the grass. The sky is that wonderful crisp shade of blue it becomes in the autumn, and every once in a while a flock of geese flies through it on their way to wherever they go.

I pull myself away from the window and stare again at the computer. I really have to get some of this stuff done before Jack picks me up tonight. I stand up and walk around the room, rubbing my hands through my hair. I kick at a shoe left lying in the middle of the room and it rolls under my unmade bed.

Muttering to myself, I get down on the floor

and reach under the bed to retrieve the shoe. *When was the last time I cleaned under here?* I wonder as I pull out a sock and a belt. I reach under again, still hunting for the shoe, and my fingers touch a sharp-edged piece of paper. Frowning, I pull my hand out and open it to see a small, yellow fluorescent star.

I sit up slowly and lean back against the edge of the bed, staring at the ceiling star. I gently touch the bent points, smoothing them as best I can. I draw my knees up to my chest and rest my cheek on them, still looking at the star.

I haven't spoken to Danelle since that night on Lions Gate Bridge. I've heard that she spent some time in the hospital after her bungee-jumping experiment failed. I've also heard that she is repeating grade twelve. But that is all I know.

I get up and close my blinds and curtains, shut off the light. It isn't really dark enough, but the little star does give off a faint yellow glow. I smile, remembering the two of us lying side by side on my bed staring up at my galaxy. But then all the other stuff comes flooding back to me — the lies, broken promises, crazy behaviour, disappearing, suicide attempt — and I crumple the innocent star in my palm.

In the months after Danelle's bungee jumping attempt, I tried hard not to think about her. It just hurt too much. Now I sit down at my computer and stare at the blank screen. Soon words like *anger* and *grief*, *gratitude* and *denial*, *sacrifice* and *loss* start filling the page. I don't know where I'm going with it, though, this letter or whatever it is, and my hands fall still.

All I ever wanted was my best friend back, but it's not that simple anymore. There is so much to say, and I don't even know where to start.

* * *

The letter appears in my mailbox one afternoon the following spring. I come home from classes and find it with the other pieces of mail, folded tightly into a little square. I sit at the kitchen table and slowly unfold it, smoothing the paper enough to read. The handwriting is familiar.

Dear Chris; It's been a while, eh? I've been trying to write this letter for a long time now, but never can quite get it written. Or if I write it, I can't bring myself to send it. I pulled a lot of crap with you. Crap you put up with, amazingly. I wanted to thank you for that. For being such a friend. Even at the last, when I was screaming at you, you were being a friend. I was just too screwed up to know it. I wanted you to know I appreciate all of it. It's taken a long, long time and it wasn't easy, but they've finally slapped a label on me, Chris, and doped me up. And, amazingly, I feel a lot better. It isn't perfect, but it is better. I hope you'll believe me when

I tell you that. I hope all is well with you. I know you are busy with school and that you and Jack are still together. He's a good guy. Take care of yourself. D

I stare at the letter for a long time, stare until the words blur and run together. I smooth the paper with my fingers, feeling Danelle in the fibres, hearing her voice in every word. It has been a long time — too long? I read the letter again, thinking of so many things, remembering so many emotions and heartaches. Then I see that she has included her phone number, and surrounding the numbers is a circle of tiny fluorescent stars. And I smile.